Gideon's face inched closer to hers

Simone could see his lip was bleeding from his fight with the mystery intruder.

She trembled.

Anticipation warred with dread.

One kiss could be deadly, she told herself. She couldn't trust him.

But when his mouth lightly touched hers, the metallic taste of blood sparked something so primal and so deep in her, she moaned into his mouth and parted her lips. All the invitation he needed to crush her to him and to invade her mouth as if all the years apart hadn't passed.

As if she was still a teenager dazed by first love.

As if he hadn't betrayed her by taking away her father.

The reminder of what had come between them chilled her inside. Just as the elevator car came to a stop and the doors opened, Simone twisted out of his arms and ran.

RED CARPET CHRISTMAS

PATRICIA ROSEMOOR

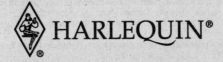

TORONTO • NEW YORK • LONDON
AMSTERDAM • PARIS • SYDNEY • HAMBURG
STOCKHOLM • ATHENS • TOKYO • MILAN • MADRID
PRAGUE • WARSAW • BUDAPEST • AUCKLAND

To my father, Walter H. Pinianski, who lost his life
to a home intruder; and to my husband, Edward,
who is still fighting for his own life. You were both on
my mind and in my heart with every word I wrote.

ISBN 0-373-22881-3

RED CARPET CHRISTMAS

Copyright © 2005 by Patricia Pinianski

www.eHarlequin.com

Printed in U.O.A.

ABOUT THE AUTHOR

Patricia Rosemoor has always had a fascination with dangerous love. In addition to her more than forty Intrigue novels, she also writes for Harlequin Blaze and Silhouette Bombshell, bringing a different mix of thrills and chills and romance to each line.

She's won a Golden Heart from Romance Writers of America and Reviewers' Choice and Career Achievement Awards from *Romantic Times* BOOKclub, and she teaches writing popular fiction and suspense-thriller writing in the fiction writing department of Columbia College Chicago. Check out her Web site: www.PatriciaRosemoor.com. You can contact Patricia either via e-mail at Patricia@PatriciaRosemoor.com, or through the publisher at Patricia Rosemoor, c/o Harlequin/Silhouette Books, 233 Broadway, New York, NY 10279.

Books by Patricia Rosemoor

CAST OF CHARACTERS

Gideon—The secretive owner of Club Undercover has spent half his life running, but now the past—and the woman he once loved—are about to catch up to him.

Simone Burke—The chief suspect in the murder of her late husband's law partner, she must turn to the man she never wanted to see again, to help clear her name.

Al Cecchi—What made someone want to kill him?

Teresa Cecchi—Did Al's widow figure out he was cheating on her?

Nikki Albright—She was a suspect until she ended up dead.

Sam Albright—Was Nikki's controlling ex-husband the secret link between the two murders?

Michael DeNali—Had Simone's brother tried to get Cecchi to pay money he owed her?

Ulf Nachtmann—Why was Simone's brother's bodyguard sneaking around and spying on her?

Galen O'Neil—Did the silent auction chair have reason to silence Al Cecchi?

Josie Ralston—What did Al's mistress know about his secrets?

Prologue

"I know about the tape. I want to hear your side of the story."

Those words had nearly choked him, David Burke thought as he headed home. Speeding north on Lake Shore Drive, he turned on his brights to cut through the fog rising from the lake. Late spring along Chicago's lakefront often brought rain and fog, and road conditions on this night were particularly treacherous.

The middle of the night hadn't been the best time for a confrontation, but when would have been? He never should have listened to the tape. What he'd learned from it was still eating at him.

Too bad he hadn't gotten a straight answer.

Rain splattered his windshield and he turned the wipers from Intermittent to Low. He would be glad when he got home to Simone's comforting arms...not that he could tell her what had happened.

As a lawyer, David was used to clients evading the truth. Normally, he was able to cut through the bull.

He'd recognized evasions and half-truths when he'd heard them, but what was he going to do about it?

Nothing was the appropriate answer, but in this case, it was one he didn't like. Too close to home.

Halfway past Grant Park, he noticed headlights in his rearview mirror. Another vehicle was following too close for the conditions. The road was slick from rain, and the fog continued to roll over the Drive in waves.

"Did your mother raise you to be an idiot?" he muttered.

Hardly anyone else was on the road at this time of night. The idiot driver had three other clear lanes, but his headlights stayed smack in the middle of David's mirror.

David cursed and shifted one lane to the right.

So did the other vehicle.

David switched back to the left.

The headlights followed him.

"What the hell?"

His chest tightened. He knew in his gut this was no coincidence. The confrontation had been a mistake. Approaching the curve before Navy Pier, he pressed the accelerator and began calculating how far it was to the next exit—about a mile and a half—and where he could go once he got off the Drive. Maybe he could disappear somewhere in Lincoln Park.

If he got off in one piece…

Without warning, the other vehicle rammed him hard. David jerked in his seat but hung on as his car's tires slid on the wet pavement.

Another hit.

Panicked, David floored the accelerator and prayed he could get home to his family...

Another hit from the other vehicle—this one far harder than the first. His car skidded and was hit again so fast and hard that it went sliding sideways, crumpling the guardrail as if it were paper.

For a moment, he was flying. Then he plummeted, the car flipping like a carnival ride in a shower of sparks toward the lake.

David closed his eyes and thought of Simone and Drew before the water claimed him.

Chapter One

Eight months later

"The Chicago Philanthropic Club is different from other charitable organizations," Simone Burke told the reporter during an interview at Red Carpet Christmas, her organization's annual holiday fund-raising event.

"Every public relations maven says the same thing about her organization," the reporter said.

Maven? An image of a much more mature woman popped into Simone's head.

"We award money for worthy projects, yes, but we don't actually cut a check for the organization," Simone said. "Instead, we pay the vendors directly. That way, money can't be redirected away from the approved project. Ah, but there's our fearless leader, Lulu Hutton—she's the one next to the Christmas tree." She motioned to catch the attention of the silver-haired matriarch who wore her age and money with class. "I'm sure she would like to speak with you."

Simone's smile stayed plastered to her face until the

reporter crossed Club Undercover's upper level where the items for the silent auction were laid out, mostly on tables decorated with holly and big red bows and branches of pine. The request for this year's auction items—give up something you love for charity.

The party was just beginning, but already the main floor of the club below was filled with Chicago's rich and famous—those who could afford the three-hundred-dollar-a-person entry. Twinkling lights embellished the club's red-and-blue neon decor, and music echoed in the cavernous space. Glancing back to see the reporter engrossed in her conversation with the organization's chairwoman, Simone finally took a deep breath and let down her guard.

Doing her best to get back into the swing of things eight months after her husband's death was every bit as difficult as she'd imagined it would be. She could get her mind on other things successfully as long as she was interacting with someone. But the moment she was alone, the worries and questions resurfaced.

David had said he was going to be late because of a case that needed his attention. Used to the hours of a successful criminal lawyer, Simone had gone to bed without him. Only to be awakened at dawn by a life-changing phone call. Someone had spotted the rear end of David's car sticking out of the lake. Trapped by his seat belt and a smashed-in car door, her husband had drowned.

According to the authorities, the weather had been bad, and David had been speeding. His car had spun out of control. Police suspected there might have been a collision—scrapings of black paint from another vehicle found on David's car might have been the result of a sideswipe in a parking lot or on the street. Or maybe it had been a hit-and-run on the expressway. With no witnesses, no other proof of another vehicle's involvement, the authorities had ruled the tragedy an accident.

As far as the insurance company was concerned, though, the jury was still out.

Simone couldn't believe fate would have taken away her best friend and the best father a woman could wish for her son. Perhaps she felt guilty that she hadn't loved him better, at least not in the way he'd wanted. Not in the romantic way he'd loved her all these years.

She'd had that once, but that had been another lifetime ago.

"You're sad. Is there something I can do to help?"

Simone turned to look at the striking woman who seemed to have appeared from nowhere. Tall and statuesque with shoulder-length mahogany hair, she wore a barely-there crimson dress with stilettos to match.

"I'm fine," Simone told her. "Just too much on my mind."

"Yes…" the woman said. "I can see that. I'm the club's hostess, Cassandra Freed. Cass." She aimed a hand with scarlet nails at Simone. "If there's anything I can do for you…"

"Simone Burke, public relations."

When she shook the hostess's hand, an odd sensation shot through Simone. Something about the way Cass was looking at her so closely made her uneasy, so she quickly withdrew her hand.

"If I think of anything," Simone said, "I'll let you know." Then the significance of that name hit her. "Cassandra Freed...aren't you the woman who made it possible for us to have our fund-raiser at this club? I heard the owner wasn't crazy about the idea."

Cass grinned. "It took a little convincing, but Gideon agreed when he heard that you plan to support Umbrella House," she said.

Umbrella House was a shelter for abused women and their children, and it was one of the primary organizations scheduled to benefit from the fund-raiser.

"This Gideon sounds like a man with a conscience."

"And a good heart," Cass said, then shifted gears. "You didn't come for a look-see at the club with the rest of the committee."

"I had a last-minute situation with my son Drew," Simone lied. "Teenagers can be quite a handful."

No way did she want to admit she'd been on an interview for a job she wasn't going to get.

"Drew," Cass mused.

The club's hostess had that look again, as if she wanted to say something about him.

Uncomfortable, Simone said, "I heard there were a few last-minute donations for the silent auction. I thought I would check to see what they were."

Smiling, she stepped away from the hostess, thinking that was the end of that.

But Cass joined her. "Some very generous contributions."

They passed a table holding a large basket of fine wines from a man's personal cellar, a pair of South Sea black pearl earrings displayed in a shell from a woman's inherited jewelry collection, a brochure to the hottest new resort on Paradise Island—the auction item was a vacation for two that a couple had meant to take themselves.

All items were supposed to mean something personal to the giver, expressing the true spirit of Christmas.

"Ooh, something I would like to own myself." Cass pointed to an Erte collar necklace of gold and diamonds, unusual because the centerpiece could be removed and worn as a brooch. She picked up the card and sighed. "Two thousand's the starting bid. A tad out of my price range."

All of the items were pricey. The club had provided security guards—two men dressed in green elf costumes milled about the room. Plus the bartender serving drinks at the nearby bar appeared formidable, as well. Perhaps of Native American ancestry, with coppery skin and hawk-like features, the man wore his long black hair pulled back and tied at his neck with a leather thong. No one was going to steal anything on his watch, Simone thought.

Most of the items to be auctioned were small, but a few pieces weren't table-friendly. A Tiffany floor lamp from someone's living room threw soft light across one end of the balcony; a narrow Victorian desk from another person's office stood sentry at the other.

"I haven't seen that before." Simone approached the burr walnut piano-top davenport desk that had been one of the late donations. The piece was only two feet wide, and she had the perfect spot for it in her living room. "I would love to bid on that piece."

If she could afford it, of course, which was unlikely considering her circumstances.

Simone opened the top to find a tooled red leather insert on an adjustable ratchet slope. She figured a hidden catch would release a secret storage compartment—common to this type of desk—but she couldn't immediately find it. Then she checked the descriptive card and realized the bidding started at $3,500. Definitely out of her price range.

She saw that Nikki Albright, a new divorcée with an apparently generous settlement, had already made the first bid.

Sighing, Simone closed the top, then noted the desk had been donated by Teresa Cecchi, wife of the man who'd been David's law partner.

She felt some resentment, but thinking about Al Cecchi would only spoil her evening, so Simone put him out of mind. If she was lucky, she wouldn't run into him this evening. She glanced over at Cass, who was staring at her strangely until something on the floor below drew the hostess's attention away from her.

"Oops, the boss wants to see me. Nice meeting you, Simone," Cass said, heading for the stairs. "Remember, if you need anything, tell any of the wait staff or bartenders, and if they can't help you, they'll let me know."

"I'll keep that in mind. Thanks."

She turned to look over the crowd in time to hear an angry voice demand "Where the hell is Galen?"

Great. Al Cecchi. And he sounded angry.

Galen O'Neill, chair of the silent auction, stood frozen in the middle of the room. In her forties, Galen was a pretty, petite woman with dark red hair, green eyes and skin that normally glowed with color. As Al Cecchi cut through the crowd toward her, Simone noticed the woman turn ashen.

Al wasn't a particularly big man—his ego was the biggest thing about him—but he could be intimidating.

"What is it, Albert?" Galen asked, sounding choked.

"The desk." Al's olive skin darkened all the way up his receding hairline, making his already sharp features even less appealing. "It's mine!"

"Um, yes, keeping with the theme of giving up something that means something to you. So generous—"

"I want it back!"

Galen started. "Um, you'll have to take that up with your wife, since she's the one who actually donated it. I saw Teresa just a while ago..." She was looking around, her manner desperate.

"Take the damn sign off the desk!" Al shouted. "It's not for sale!"

"But Teresa *gave* it to us," Galen argued.

"Because she was angry with me. And delusional!

That desk was my mother's. Teresa's trying to get back at me by giving it away!"

"Please, Albert, don't make a scene."

Indeed, everyone in the area seemed to be focused on the argument.

"I don't care who hears me! I will hold you personally responsible if I don't get Mama's desk back!"

Galen was shaking as she said, "I—I'm afraid you'll have to bid on it."

"Fine!" Al stormed over to the desk, practically running into Simone. She moved out of the way, and he picked up a pen and quickly scribbled his bid. "That should do it until I find Teresa and get this straightened out."

"Really, there is no way to get the desk back other than win the bid," Galen squeaked to his retreating back.

"You won't let someone else have it if you know what's good for you!"

Simone had no doubt Al would try to circumvent paying for the desk. He was the antithesis of generous, as she well knew. He was refusing to release any money—David's share of the law firm—to her. She was certain Al would try to find a way to negate the small fortune David had brought into the business before he'd died, thereby cutting her out completely. She suspected she might have to hire a lawyer of her own to get what Al owed her and Drew.

If she was a different type of person, she would simply sic her brother Michael on him. For the first time in her life, she was tempted to use her family connections.

Before Simone could move away, another member of the Philanthropic Club, Nikki Albright—Marilyn-blond and statuesque in a gold lamé number—slithered over to the desk and scribbled another bid. "If Cecchi thinks he's getting this desk back, he's got another think coming," she told anyone within earshot. "I don't care how much I have to bid to keep it away from him!"

Nikki's bitter tone made Simone wonder what Al had done to *her*. "I'm sure it will all work out for the best," she murmured.

"You ought to watch your mouth, my dear," a man said in a low, cultured voice.

Simone recognized Nikki's ex-husband. Sam Albright wore a perfectly tailored gray suit, the cut of his blond hair making him look distinguished.

"Why? What are you going to do to stop me from talking, Sammy?" Nikki demanded, pushing her way past him.

"I'm not beyond finding ways of dealing with unpleasant situations," he warned. "You've had a taste of that before."

He watched her through narrowed blue eyes for a moment before shaking his head and moving on. Nikki looked genuinely frightened.

Simone rubbed a chill from her arms. What a bully. She made her way downstairs, looking for reporters and intending to steer clear of them. On the main level, guests gathered in small groups, sat at tables or boogied on the dance floor.

At least half of the crowd was middle-aged or older so the deejay was playing old seventies' rock tunes. Simone liked the music better than the incessant hip-hop that used to come from Drew's room at all hours. Her son had been driving her crazy with his music until she'd cut a deal with him that he would wear headphones when she was home.

Halfway down the open-backed staircase, Simone stopped when she spotted Cass talking to a man who looked disturbingly familiar. This must be the boss the hostess had mentioned. He was tall and muscular and handsome. Even from a distance she could see his chiseled features framed by slicked blue-black hair. Her stomach knotted and her throat tightened.

He looked like a mature version of...

She forced herself to continue down the stairs, only she couldn't take her eyes off the man. Before she reached the club floor—as if he knew she was staring at him—he lifted his face and met her gaze.

A wave of dizziness swept through her and almost made her stumble.

Cass was pulling the man toward her and all Simone wanted to do was escape.

She could see Cass's mouth moving—the hostess was obviously trying to tell her something. But the blood was rushing through Simone's head and she could only distinguish one word.

"Gideon."

GIDEON WAS stunned.

The sounds and movement of the club receded as he came face-to-face with the woman he'd thought was out of his life forever.

He couldn't stop staring at Simone. She'd matured into an exquisite beauty. Her dark hair hung in long waves over her dark green gown—the same startling green as her eyes.

Taking the final step down toward him, Simone held on to the railing as if to steady herself. She was taller than Gideon remembered, maybe five feet eight or nine, and her curves had matured—full breasts, trim waist, round hips.

It really was *his* Simone. He'd known her as Simone DeNali, not Simone Burke.

"Mrs. Burke," he said, trying to keep his voice pleasantly neutral as he glanced at her left hand, which had a white-knuckled grip on the railing.

No wedding ring...

So she'd removed it.

"Is there something I should know?" Cass asked, looking from him to Simone.

"I imagine if there were, you would already know it," he said casually.

Cass sighed. "How many times do I have to tell you it doesn't work that way?"

Simone blinked and seemed confused. "What doesn't work what way?"

"Cass's—"

"Intuition," the hostess finished for him, then rushed

on to add, "Simone is the public relations person for the Chicago Philanthropic Club."

"And doing a fine job as far as I can see." He didn't take his gaze off Simone.

"How would you know what kind of a job I'm doing, considering we just met?" Simone asked.

Her familiar low, throaty voice made the skin along his forearms prickle with goose bumps. That voice had always turned him on. Now here she was challenging him, Gideon realized, trying to get him to say something to admit they knew each other.

Or was she?

"It was lovely meeting you, Gideon," Simone said, suddenly seeming distracted. "Congratulations on the success of Club Undercover." Her smile didn't reach her eyes when she said, "If you'll excuse me, I need to circulate."

She floated off into the crowd without so much as a glance back his way.

"What was that all about?" Cass asked.

"If you don't have anything to keep you busy, I'm sure I could find something."

"Uh, right, I get the hint. But if you want to talk about her…"

Gideon didn't answer and Cass didn't wait around for another invitation to leave. The second she moved off, Gideon tried to find Simone in the crowd, but she seemed to have disappeared.

Again…

She could destroy everything he'd worked for. She could destroy *him*.

All she had to do was tell her brother, Mob boss Michael DeNali, that he'd returned to Chicago. Michael had sworn to kill him before he'd disappeared several lifetimes ago.

But he wasn't running anymore, not ever again.

Chapter Two

Simone rushed through the crowd to head off her brother before he came face-to-face with the owner of the club. Joey Ruscetti might call himself Gideon, but that didn't mean Michael wouldn't recognize him. Her pulse ratcheted up a notch. She prayed Gideon wasn't following her. She chanced a look back but didn't see him.

"Simone, there you are."

Michael wrapped an arm around her back and kissed her cheek. Dressed in Armani, his hair fashionably spiked, he almost blended in with the crowd. But there was something about him—the way he carried himself, the way his dark eyes continually scanned the club as if looking for enemies—that set him apart. Not to mention the muscular bodyguard who stood several paces away. Big and blond, Ulf Nachtmann had the attention of several interested women, but his pale blue eyes were focused on the man he'd been paid to keep safe.

"You don't have a drink," he said.

"I'm working, remember?"

"Your work here is done. This party's a success. You should be celebrating."

Not anymore, she thought.

Michael grabbed a flute of bubbly from a passing waiter's tray and placed it in her hand. "To my little sister's success."

"I didn't put this fund-raiser together myself, you know. I'm just one cog in the machine."

"Then to success in any venture. How did your little job interview go?"

Simone bit back a sharp retort. Being the public relations person for a local Chicago-based charity might be small potatoes to him, but it would have been a big deal to her. "It could have gone better."

In the eyes of the man who'd interviewed her, the voluntary charity work she'd done year after year hadn't made up for her not having had a paying job.

Michael slugged down his drink and said, "I don't know why you suddenly want to work anyway."

"I have a son to raise, remember? Who knows if I'll ever see a penny of David's life insurance."

David had taken out a two-million-dollar policy several months before his death. The insurance investigator was of the opinion that David might have committed suicide. Ridiculous! Then what?

Simone wanted to believe her husband's death had been an accident.

So why couldn't she?

"The insurance money'll come through eventually," Michael reassured her.

"In the meantime, it would be nice if I could get David's share of Cecchi and Burke."

"If Cecchi needs some incentive—"

"No. And that's final."

"All right. Don't get yourself into a twist." He signaled a waiter and pointed to his empty glass. "And don't worry about the money. I'll give you whatever you need. Even better, sell your place and move in with me. Since the divorce, that place is too big for me. I rattle around all by myself."

Him, his staff and his bodyguards, Simone thought, but she knew what he meant.

The Prairie Avenue mansion, built at the start of the twentieth century by a leading industrialist, had been too big for their family when they'd all lived there. It had always been a showplace rather than a home. After their father had been incarcerated at Stateville Correctional Center in Joliet, their mother had left it for their town house in Florida. And there she'd stayed. Michael had refused to move. He'd hung on to the place through three divorces.

She and Michael had been close as kids. He'd always turned to her to feel better when he'd screwed up and Papa had been hard on him. And after Papa had been indicted, Michael had assumed the responsibility of being the head of the family. He'd seen her through a rough time and had made sure she was protected, just as she used to do for him.

"You and Drew can have the whole third floor to yourselves," Michael said. "Think about it. David isn't around anymore, but Drew still needs a man's hand."

Her teenage son could use a good male influence. Michael just didn't happen to be it.

Drew still hadn't gotten over David's death. The sixteen-year-old was already looking more and more to Michael for guidance.

That's what Simone feared most.

Realizing her brother was still waiting for an answer, Simone said, "You know how I feel about taking money from you, Michael."

"It's *family* money."

"Exactly."

His visage darkened and he said, "I run legitimate businesses, Simone."

Some were, perhaps, but Simone didn't believe he'd divested himself of certain edgy if lucrative ventures that included an escort service staffed by gorgeous women and a security outfit with specialists who looked as if they'd pumped iron behind bars.

"I need to know I can take care of Drew and me, Michael. I need to prove this to myself." Papa had taken care of her, then Michael, then David. It was her turn to take care of herself. "I need purpose to my life, I need something that someone didn't give me. Surely you can understand that—wanting to have something you call your own."

His glower softened and he pulled out a pack of cigarettes and shook one free. "Okay, okay, little sister. You always wow me, you know. We'll do it your way for now." A book of matches in his left hand, he bent a single match and touched the head to the flint. He flicked with his thumb and the match flamed to life. "But you change your mind and want me to take care of Cecchi, you just say the word."

She would never tell Michael to act for her. Hoping to smooth over the atmosphere between them, she asked, "So, where's your date for the evening?"

After taking a long drag on his cigarette, Michael said, "Don't have one. The society dames who are here are rich. You're the only woman who's ever loved me without wanting anything from me. Hell, you won't take it when I offer. Maybe that's the key to getting a keeper—getting someone like you, a woman who won't want to be with me just for the money."

Simone smiled. Of course, Michael wasn't here because the holiday spirit had hit him. He would never even wear a sprig of holly or a decorative tie during the season…not even when she bought one for him. Even when they'd been kids, he'd said pretending to believe in Santa was only good for the loot you got. So he wanted Santa to give him a new wife?

"There are plenty of eligible women around."

"And I see one right now. Later, sis."

Focused, Michael moved in on a young woman Simone didn't recognize. With purple chunks highlighting her spiked short brown hair, and even though it was winter, wearing an unusual outfit that left her midriff bare, and her navel rings showing, she certainly stood out from the more conservative crowd.

Not exactly Michael's type, but hopefully she would keep him entertained and away from their ghost from the past.

Gideon...

"THAT BITCH made another bid?"

Having just entered the silent auction area, Gideon whipped around to see who'd made that comment and saw a thin, middle-aged man with a receding hairline adding a bid for the Victorian desk.

"I need a stiff drink," the man muttered and stalked off to get one.

Gideon signaled Blade, who was tending bar tonight, to keep an eye on the angry guest.

Then he looked around for Simone. She'd given him the slip and had stayed out of his line of sight all evening. Surely she couldn't have left, not when she was one of the society women running the show.

He'd seen Michael, though, Gideon thought grimly, thankful that he'd managed to stay off the other man's radar. He didn't want any trouble, not tonight. This charity event was too important—among the recipients of the funds raised would be a local shelter for abused women and children.

After tonight...well, Gideon didn't want any trouble with Michael DeNali at any time, but at least he would have people to watch his back.

"You must have a lot on *your* mind."

Gideon realized Gabe Connor, his security chief, was standing directly in front of him. His narrowed green eyes, intent expression and hard-set square jaw stood in contrast to the fantasy of the Santa hat covering his dark hair.

"It's turned out to be an unusual evening, all right," Gideon admitted. "I've just seen a couple of ghosts from the past."

"Anything you want me to do?"

Gideon noticed a blonde stopping at the Victorian desk and adding a bid to the list. The one dueling for the piece with the man at the bar?

Realizing Gabe was waiting, he snapped his attention back to the man. "Ever heard of Michael DeNali?"

"Who hasn't? He's *here* tonight?"

Gideon nodded, brought Gabe over to the balcony railing, spotted Michael in the crowd and pointed him out. "He's trouble, and I don't want trouble out of control in my club."

"I'll get right on it."

Though Gabe was dressed as well as any guest, the headset threaded under the Santa hat kept him in contact with his team and identified him as security. He used the system now to talk to one of the men on the main floor and instructed him to keep an eye on Michael.

"Is this something we should talk about?" Gabe then asked.

"Maybe another day."

Gideon was aware of the curiosity he inspired in Team Undercover, as he liked to call his associates. They knew nothing about his past, but it seemed his past had just caught up with him.

Isn't that why he'd come back to Chicago?

No matter that he'd spent half his life running—and despite Michael's threats of vengeance—he'd always known he would have to come back to face what he'd left behind. It was a matter of honor. Besides which, he hadn't been able to get Simone out of his blood, and to do that, he knew would have to confront her one day.

But after having reclaimed the city for his own and after having had a local private eye investigate Simone and her new life, he'd kept a low profile and had waited for the right moment, the right opportunity to…

To what?

He'd never quite figured that out. Simone had been happily married with a son, and so he'd been tempted to leave until he'd found his mission, a reason for being. A reason for staying put and not moving on to the next city, the next meaningless life, as he'd done over and over through the years.

Team Undercover—they'd all worked together several times now to help people out of dire straits. When the desperate had nowhere else to turn, they could turn to him and his associates. It was the reason that, in the end, he'd agreed to the charity event at Club Under-cover. Giving aid to abused women and their kids fit right in with the team's mission.

But no one on the team knew Gideon's true identity. Maybe it was time to break the silence.

When the desperate had nowhere else to turn...

He only hoped that didn't end up being him.

"You HAVE five minutes to make your final bids," came the announcement over the loudspeakers in the club. "This is the five-minute warning."

Simone entered the now-crowded silent auction. People were jockeying to make their final bids. She scanned the crowd for a dark head that stood out above the others. No Gideon. She didn't know if she was disappointed or relieved.

A loud "Oops" turned her toward Galen O'Neill, who'd dropped something that went skittering toward Simone.

"I'll get it." Simone squeezed past a couple of men and picked up a fancy curved dagger. She took a moment to admire the hilt, richly decorated in antique gold with a large garnet in the pommel, before returning it to the table. "Wow, that's some weapon."

"William has a collection of old weapons," the auction chairwoman said of her husband. "I'm hoping to give this one to him as a Christmas gift. It's a ceremonial dagger. The blade even has a blood groove."

Too much information. She'd never noticed Galen's bloodthirsty side before. Normally the auction chairwoman seemed, well, timid. At the moment, with her eyes glittering and her cheeks flushed, Galen seemed anything but.

"Here's hoping you win the bid," Simone said.

Spotting Al Cecchi across the room, she noted the lawyer had caught up to his wife. Teresa Cecchi looked stiff with anger as she straightened the peplum of her Christmas-red suit. Simone figured she'd better try to smooth things over between the couple before the argument drew notice. She didn't want any negative press to spoil the success of the evening.

"You're delusional!" Al was saying loud enough for Simone to hear as she approached.

"I know what I know, Albert. I smelled perfume on your jacket."

"Perfume I was buying you for Christmas. But you decided I had a mistress and gave away Mama's desk! I need to make my final bid to get it back."

Teresa stormed away. Al turned and practically ran into Simone.

"What the hell do you want?" he demanded.

"Only what's ours." Simone hadn't meant to speak to him about the money in public, for heaven's sake. The words just seemed to slip out of her. Embarrassed, she lowered her voice. "We need to talk about the business, Al. Not here, but soon. I have a son to support."

"I told you to wait until the fiscal year ends."

"Why are you stalling?" Something he'd been doing for eight months now.

"I don't have time for this!"

Before Al could get past her, an amplified voice said, "All bids are now closed."

"What?" His face darkened as he turned to Simone.

"I lost Mama's desk because of you!" He gave her a shove that made her stumble backward.

Catching herself, she gasped, "How dare you!"

He shoved her a second time.

Temper flaring, she said, "Touch me again and you'll regret it!"

Suddenly realizing that several sets of eyes were on them and embarrassed by her public outburst, Simone shrank from the angry lawyer, who turned back to the bar and ordered a double scotch. Though she could use a drink herself, Simone knew that wouldn't be wise. A private person, she would never choose to air her dirty laundry in public. No doubt that champagne had loosened her tongue.

Not wanting to see any questioning gazes on her, Simone looked straight ahead as she made her way through the crowd to the ladies' room to calm down. She felt eyes following her around the end of the bar. No doubt Al was staring daggers at her. She glanced back, but he was gone. In her moment of inattention, she rammed into a big pillowy body in a red suit.

"Ho! Ho! Ho!"

"Sorry, Santa," she muttered, head down as she hurried into the hallway.

A woman was coming out of the ladies' room, a pretty space decorated in the blues and reds of the club. Thankfully, it was empty. After freshening up, Simone took a seat on an upholstered stool in front of a mirror, where she spent an inordinate amount of time fussing with her long dark hair and re-applying some gold eye shadow that made the green of her eyes sparkle. Anything to postpone going back into the club proper. If she were lucky, Al would be gone when she rejoined the party.

Not that it felt much like a party to her anymore. Between seeing the ghost from her past and being confronted by the bane of her present, all she felt was stressed out.

Closing her eyes for a moment, Simone breathed deeply and slowly, tried to use the meditation technique she'd learned to help her after she'd lost her husband. But rather than calming her, the technique brought to mind an image that made her pulse race—a handsome face framed by slick blue-black hair.

The face of the man who had broken her heart.

If she did nothing, if she walked away from the club and never came back, would it be over then?

It had to be. She couldn't go back in time. He wouldn't want to.

What was he even doing here in Chicago?

Did he have a death wish?

As the questions crowded her mind, Simone realized this wasn't making her feel any better. She needed to come out of hiding and find some pleasant company until the end of the evening.

Simone opened the door and took a step out, but her foot caught on something. She staggered back and looked down. In the split second it took her to process what she was seeing, her heart raced into overdrive.

Before she could say anything or call anyone, a

woman's scream froze her in place. Nikki Albright was standing at the opening to the hallway, staring at her, eyes wide. Behind her, several people hurriedly gathered.

"Is he dead?" someone asked.

"I'm a doctor," a man said and pushed into the hall. He knelt at Al Cecchi's side and felt for a pulse. A jeweled dagger was sticking out of Al's chest.

Chapter Three

"She killed him!" Nikki Albright gasped when the doctor had declared the lawyer dead. Turning to the people behind her, she yelled, "Simone Burke killed Al Cecchi!"

"What?" Simone's heart felt as if it were slamming against her ribs. "No! I didn't kill anyone!"

Guests crowded the opening to the hallway. All eyes on her were either accusing or suspicious. The already narrow space became claustrophobic, making Simone feel as if she were trapped in a jail cell, which—if the police believed Nikki—would be her next address.

"All right, everyone back off. No one leaves until the police get here! Gabe, you secure the area. Have your men secure the exits."

Through a haze of fear, Simone heard the familiar voice issue orders.

This couldn't be happening to her; it just couldn't. She was the DeNali who'd broken the mold, the first DeNali in four generations to turn away from the family business. Her father was still paying for his crimes, though he'd been incarcerated for one he hadn't committed.

But who would believe her?

"Come on, let's go to my office."

Gideon held out a hand to her.

Throat tight, she ignored the offer and, spine stiff, walked past him. He was right behind her, his voice low, speaking for her ears only.

"Head for the stairs, Simone. Go down and then across the club floor to the main entrance. My office is on the other side of the foyer."

Simone stared straight ahead. Tunnel vision. Ears blocked to the cacophony of voices around her. She ignored the questions directed at her by a reporter. Gideon used his body as a barrier so the woman couldn't get too close.

It had been nearly two decades since she'd felt so vulnerable, pummeling her with questions she couldn't answer about her father who'd just been indicted for a murder he swore he hadn't committed.

She'd struck out at one of them in fury, had ripped the mike from his hands and had hit the guy in the head with his equipment. Her brother Michael had saved her that day. He'd pulled her away from the crowd before she could do more damage. Later, he'd made some financial settlement that had made the charges against her for aggravated battery disappear.

Michael...where was he?

Descending the stairs, Simone looked around wildly

for her brother, but she couldn't spot him in the crowd
below.

*Had Michael settled with Cecchi for her as he'd
threatened to do?*

Dear Lord, surely not!

Glancing back to look for her brother on the upper
floor, she almost missed a stair. A large hand grasped
her arm and kept her from falling.

"Careful."

Careful. She had been.

All these years, she'd lived a careful life. No blem-
ishes on her record. Why would anyone believe she
could be capable of murder?

What if Nikki was covering for herself?

As they stepped foot onto the main floor of the club,
Simone realized Gideon was pressed up against her as
he tried to get her through the crowd. Despite herself…her resolve…the years spent away from
him…she felt long-repressed emotions bubble through
her. She tried not to panic, but she felt trapped—no way
to get away from him, no way out of the situation.

Is this the way Papa had felt after being convicted
of killing this man's father?

GIDEON'S HAND burned. *He* burned. After all this time
apart, he still was attracted to Simone.

When they got to his office, Simone wrenched her
arm free and, with as much dignity as she could mus-
ter, preceded him into the room.

"Sit," he said, picking up the phone and dialing

Logan's cell. He needed to talk to the member of his team who was also a Chicago police detective. Voice mail. "I need you here," was all he said.

Simone was still standing. Her eyes seemed unfocused, her thoughts turning inward. Was she thinking of him...or scrambling for an alibi?

"Why did you bring me in here?"

"I thought you would appreciate getting away from the crowd until the police arrive."

Blanching, she said, "I should appreciate that," as if she really didn't. Waves of defiance pulsed from her as she asked, "Um, what was the name again?"

"Gideon will do."

"Gideon...a far cry from Joseph Ruscetti."

Her green eyes glittered, challenging him to deny it. Which, of course, he couldn't.

He'd had many identities in the past seventeen years, but he'd never been able to forget who he was. Joseph Ruscetti, only son of mobster Frank Ruscetti, who'd been gunned down by rival Richard DeNali. Her father.

He'd witnessed the murder.

His testimony had put Simone's father away, and she'd refused to see or speak to him. Then after the trial, he, his mother and younger sister Angela had been placed in the witness protection program and been given new identities and a new home far from Chicago.

But somehow, Michael's men had closed in on his new home, and though the mobsters had been arrested—and he and his family had been moved again—

he'd known staying in one place hadn't been safe. He couldn't endanger his mother or kid sister.

At age eighteen, he'd taken off alone.

He'd changed names, occupations and cities so often that sometimes he'd had to stop to think about who and what he was supposed to be on any given day.

But now he knew exactly who he was. And he wasn't running anymore.

Simone was the question mark. Only eight months before, her husband had died under mysterious circumstances. And now her husband's law partner had been murdered.

"Did you do it?" he asked.

Glaring at him for a moment, Simone reminded him of the teenager who'd won his heart. Her defiance soon wilted, and her eyes watered. Shaking her head, she felt behind her for a chair and nearly fell into it.

"I didn't like Al Cecchi," she admitted, "but of course I didn't kill him."

She looked so out of place in his office. Her plush femininity against the stark masculinity of chrome, black furniture and deep blue walls. She belonged in a room with lush colors and soft edges.

"There's no *of course* about it," he said, cutting off his wandering thoughts. "Not to the authorities."

"Because I'm a DeNali."

"That…and because you threatened him."

Her brow wrinkled for a moment as if she didn't know what he meant. Then her expression changed to one of surprise, as if his meaning finally dawned on her.

"He shoved me. Twice. I was simply warning him to keep his hands off me."

"I heard someone say you told him he would regret it if he touched you again."

"I lost my temper."

"*Did* he touch you again?"

"No!"

"What did happen?"

Gideon watched Simone closely as she told him she'd retreated to the ladies' room to cool off and that when she'd opened the door, she'd tripped over the already-dead lawyer.

His gut told him she was telling the truth. The tightness that had gripped him inside eased a bit. He knew she wasn't like her father and brother. Call him sentimental, call him a fool, but he still believed she was the same Simone he'd once loved.

"When you were in the ladies' room, did you hear anything?"

"I—I wasn't paying attention."

"Someone gets killed right outside the door. There must have been a struggle. But you don't hear anything."

She blinked and her voice quivered as she asked, "You don't…believe me?"

"The question is, will the police believe you?"

"You don't think they will?"

"Did you have a motive?" he pressed her.

"No!"

"You said you didn't like Cecchi. Why not? He was your husband's partner."

Simone's eyes widened, and Gideon realized she was shocked. Her mind was working, putting it together.

"You knew?" she finally asked.

"I know a lot of things," he said vaguely.

Gideon knew she hadn't waited long before turning to another man and making a new life.

He knew she'd had a successful marriage and had devoted herself to her husband and son.

He knew she'd been struggling financially for months since David Burke had died in that car crash.

"You know a lot of things about me?" she asked.

"Shouldn't I?"

"For how long?"

"For as long as I've been back in Chicago." When she didn't say anything, he said, "More than a year."

"Why?"

Gideon shrugged. "Curiosity, I guess." Before she could ask him anything more, he said, "Back to Cecchi. What's the story there?"

"He owes me money."

"How much?"

Simone shrugged. "The question of the century. Half of the business. At least a million, I imagine, if his accountant ever gets around to preparing a report."

Gideon whistled. "A million. At least. And that's not much of a motive?"

Simone popped out of the leather chair. "I don't kill people!"

"You threatened—"

"To make Al regret touching me, yes." Color rose in her neck and cheeks, and her spine seemed to grow steel. "I never threatened to kill him!"

This was his Simone...the one he remembered.

Fighting the urge to take her in his arms, to crush her to him and find out if her lips still had the power to make him forget everything but her, he said, "I believe you."

"That I didn't say the words or that I didn't mean it?"

"Do you always mean what you say?" He couldn't help himself. Even though he was over it, the memory wouldn't die. She'd done a disappearing act before hearing his side of the story. "Let me think. Mmm, no."

Her expression went rigid. Obviously she knew he meant their past.

"It doesn't sound as if you believe I'm innocent," she said through stiff lips.

"I'm playing devil's advocate. You don't think the cops are going to do me one better?"

She shuddered, and he softened a little inside. He could only imagine the horror Simone felt at the possibility of being arrested.

Tried.

Convicted.

Maybe he was a fool, but he believed her story. Despite all the years that had passed and how she'd betrayed him, he couldn't let her take the fall for something she hadn't done.

AT LEAST the police hadn't arrested her.

They'd questioned her at the club along with everyone else. They'd also threatened to hold her for twenty-four hours until she'd demanded she be allowed to call a lawyer. That hadn't been necessary; at least, not yet.

Thank God for small mercies, Simone thought, pulling her car into the garage in the middle of the night. She hoped Drew was asleep. He'd known she would be late, just not how late. If he heard her come in, her son would be sure to question her. Not that she could keep this from him.

The situation was serious—she'd been told not to leave the city.

By the time she'd left Club Undercover, the news media had set up camp outside. The club was in a trendy, gentrified area of the city where things like parking lots were non-existent. She hadn't left the club alone—the benefit committee, all questioned in the same manner as she, had left as a group—so she hadn't been singled out. Galen O'Neill had been quite comforting, assuring her that she believed in Simone's innocence. Nikki Albright hadn't been so kind, but at least she'd kept her mouth shut as the detective in charge had told her to do.

Simone had been relieved as she'd sped home, Mozart blaring from her tape deck. She'd tried to lose herself in the music, but for once she couldn't forget that she'd touched the dagger. If they checked her fingerprints...

Then there was the media, who would run with the story and dig into her background.

Shuddering, Simone crossed the backyard. Her

home was a two-story greystone with other buildings abutting hers on both sides. The yard was tiny, but stretching to the lakefront, Lincoln Park was only a half block's walk away. She lived in a neighborhood of renovated nineteenth-century million-dollar-plus homes—lots of greystones and brownstones—sitting between the busy park and lively Clark Street. The main thoroughfare of the neighborhood was rife with restaurants and specialty shops.

She couldn't imagine living elsewhere.

Especially not in a jail cell.

Letting herself into the house through the kitchen—a cook's dream with an island preparation area, two sinks and enough cabinets for multiple sets of dinnerware—Simone heard voices and stiffened until she realized the living room television was on.

"Drew, honey, what are you doing up?" she asked, walking through the dining area to the front room, where the only lights came from the television and the giant Christmas tree they'd dragged home just a few days before. They hadn't even had a chance to decorate it, but they had wound several strands of lights through the branches. "It's late."

Her son was stirring from his nest on the couch. "I was trying to wait up for you, but I fell asleep."

His eyes were droopy, his hair bed-head spiked. The sight warmed Simone, but her chest tightened. "Honey, you don't have to wait up for me. Worrying is my job."

"Dad would have done it."

"You have to be at work at six in the morning."

Simone was proud of the boy who'd insisted on getting a job to help pay expenses. She'd wanted to refuse to let him do it, but then realized he was growing up and that assuming responsibility would be good for him. He was a busboy for a busy eatery on Clark Street. He worked two weekend morning shifts and two weeknight shifts and still had time to do his homework and hang out with his friends. She let him give her half his pay from each check—he'd wanted to give it all to her—and put it into an account for him. She'd told him to spend the rest of the money on himself, but she knew he was hoarding it.

Drew was so much like David.

Even though he was Gideon's son.

"WHAT TIES do you have to Simone Burke?"

"Who said I had ties?" Even now Gideon didn't feel comfortable shedding his disguise and being forthcoming, not even with a member of Team Undercover.

"Why else would you want to help her?" asked Blade, who leaned against a wall, arms crossed over his broad chest.

"Maybe I just think Simone is innocent."

Team Undercover had gathered in his office shortly after Detective John Logan had arrived. Though he was full of them now. The presence of Logan—former employee of Gideon's—had raised some questions with the detective in charge of the case, but Logan had covered by saying the owner was a friend and he was there only as an observer.

Only a few people knew of the team's existence.

"C'mon, Gideon," Cass said. "We've all trusted you with our pasts. When are you going to trust us with yours? I sensed the connection."

Gideon shrugged, unwilling to spill all. "You always sense connections."

"Only when they're real. How long have you known Simone Burke? When I introduced you, the air between you was so thick I could cut it."

"Simple attraction."

"Not so simple," Cass countered.

"Let's say it is."

Gideon could tell Cass wanted to argue with him, but for once she backed down.

Cass sighed and said, "All right. Simone Burke is no murderer—that much I know."

"And that's all anyone has to know."

"Then who did murder Cecchi?" Gabe asked.

"The question Team Undercover is going to answer," Gideon said.

But there wasn't much they could do until he got Simone's approval.

A BLANKET OF SNOW drifted down from the night sky. His thoughts filled with Simone, he drove home from the basketball game. He'd wanted to be with her, but she'd said not tonight. She'd acted as if she'd had something important on her mind. She'd even said she needed to talk to him privately, but in the end she'd clammed up. Not enough time, she'd said after checking her watch.

She'd kissed him hard and fast and had been out of the car before he'd been able to get his hands on her.

So he wondered all the way home: was she finally going to tell him that she was ready for a permanent commitment?

If his buddies knew how much he wanted to hear those words pass her lips, they would laugh at him. Love is for fools. Get what you can and go on to the next girl. *That's what they would say.*

He shook his head. He didn't want another girl. Simone was the only one for him.

But what if it wasn't that? What if she wanted to tell him something he didn't want to hear? Like they couldn't go on seeing one another?

Chest tight, stomach knotted, he worried she might break up to try to be noble. In the process of applying to colleges, he was dragging his heels, and she knew it. He didn't want to leave Chicago, not if it meant being separated from the girl he loved.

He turned down his street, tight with white-shrouded cars, near-impassable with snow that hadn't yet been plowed or salted. No parking on the Gold Coast. Big surprise. Luckily his family had an old carriage house out back big enough for three cars.

He saw a car—one he didn't recognize—sitting in front of his garage. The motor was running, but it wasn't moving.

He remained at the mouth of the alley, waiting. If the other car was stuck, that was it. He'd have to back out and find some other place to park.

Even as he thought it, he saw movement. He wiped the inside of the foggy windshield for a clearer view and realized his father was out there by the garage talking with another man in an overcoat and wide-brimmed hat. The man turned his head slightly and his dark-framed glasses caught the light.

Richard DeNali. What was Simone's father doing here?

Joey gripped the steering wheel and wondered if he should back out of the alley. What if they had business? Pop kept business and family separate. No bodyguards, though. Maybe the business was personal. Him and Simone.

What if that's what she'd been trying to tell him—that her father was doing something to stop them from seeing each other? Their fathers had been rivals for years.

He began to sweat, but decided he wouldn't run away like some kid. At seventeen, he was a man and would take responsibility for his actions. And for his future.

Before he could get out of the car, a blue flash startled him and froze him to his seat. Another flash. No sound. His father swayed forward and fell into the snow. Still holding his gun, DeNali put a cigarette in his mouth and lit it one-handed before getting into the dark sedan.

Heart pounding, Joey threw open the door and lunged out. "Pop!" he yelled, his feet chunking into the drift, then slipping and sliding on the ice beneath the new snow.

The dark car pulled down the alley.

His eyes flicked to the license plate—RDN 1—before he dropped to the ground next to his father who lay still on his side, a pool of blood making a widening circle in the snow.

"Pop!" he cried as he turned his father onto his back. His father had been shot in the gut and the chest. "Can you hear me? Please say you can hear me!"

His father's eyes opened and slowly focused. "Joey…"

"I'll get help, Pop, I'll get someone."

But his father gripped his wrist to stop him. Rather than getting to his feet, Joey slid an arm under the broad back and lifted. His father coughed. Dark fluid bubbled up from stiff lips.

He rocked his father against him, crying, "What, Pop? What is it?"

"DeNali…"

And then his father went limp with a sigh.

"Pop, no!" he cried. "Help! Mario! Dominick! I need help!"

Sounds assaulted him—a door opening, voices, a scream—as he continued rocking his father, knowing it was already too late.

Gideon awoke in a sweat and cursed.

He hadn't had the nightmare in years. All it had taken was contact with Simone to bring it all back.

Rising naked from the bed, he moved to the windows and looked out. Fresh snow blanketed the area. This night was so like that one long ago.

What had Simone meant to tell him before leaving the car? Had she known her father meant to kill his?

He'd never been able to ask her. She'd refused to see him and then had simply disappeared.

But if she had known…

Gideon's chest tightened.

Another question that needed answering.

Chapter Four

The lion roared from his perch on one of the heated rocks in the yard outside the Lion House.

Simone wondered if he was expressing his approval of the million holiday lights illuminating the zoo or if he was protesting the lateness of the hour and the gathering crowd. For several weeks between Thanksgiving and New Year's Day, the Lincoln Park Zoo was open at night, offering special activities for the holidays. The evening's entertainment was just beginning. Loudspeakers blared Christmas music, with intermittent announcements about various family activities.

Brushing the snowflakes from the sleeve of her deep green coat, Simone checked her watch and wondered again why Gideon had insisted on seeing her today. As soon as possible. Having tried to put out of mind what had happened the night before—including her run-in with a man she never thought she'd see again—she'd spent as normal a day as possible, which meant meeting with other members of the Women's Board of the

Chicago Philanthropic Club here this afternoon as scheduled. She'd tried to use that as an excuse as to why she couldn't meet with Gideon. He'd circumvented her by insisting he would simply come to her.

Despite the boisterous guests and the old-fashioned Christmas tune blaring from the speakers, Simone was tense, wary and itching to leave. Drew would be working tonight, giving her a good opportunity to get some Christmas shopping done. Not that she was particularly in the mood, but she'd do anything to keep her mind occupied.

Damn what Gideon wanted! She'd just decided to leave when she heard his voice close behind her.

"I wasn't sure you would be here," Gideon said.

Her heart thudded as she felt his heat press against her back through her wool coat. Her stomach knotted and her chest pulled tight; she fought the reactions he'd always wrenched from her.

"I don't know why I am still here," she admitted.

"Maybe you never got over me."

That whipped her around, and she glared up into Gideon's face. "Maybe your head is too big for a hat and that's why you're not wearing one!"

He was wearing a long black wool coat with a slash of crimson at his throat, but his head was bare. Snowflakes drifted through the haze of lights to halo his dark hair. Despite the smile that quivered along his lips, there was no mistaking the powerful intensity radiating from him, making her take a step back.

"At least you don't deny it," he said.

"What is it, Gideon?" she snapped. "What do you want from me?"

Silence hung between them for a few seconds. Simone held her breath, waiting.

And then he said, "To help you."

"Help me what?"

"Prove your innocence."

"In this country, someone is innocent until proven guilty." Although injustice could be done, as she well remembered.

"That doesn't stop the state attorney's office from building a case against you."

"Just because I was angry that Al Cecchi owed me money—"

"Owed you a fortune, you mean. You argued with him just before he was murdered. What about the dagger, Simone? If they run your fingerprints, will they get a match?"

The dagger...damn! She'd almost forgotten.

If only she hadn't picked up the murder weapon when it had fallen off the auction table. She clenched her jaw. How had Gideon known about that? Or was he on a fishing expedition? Last night, when she'd told him she hadn't murdered Al, he'd said he believed her. But did he really?

"I don't have time for this."

She started to swing past him but he stretched his arm to block her, stopping her cold.

"Make time. Do you have a lawyer?"

The best criminal lawyer she'd known—the only one she'd trusted—had been her late husband, David.

"I don't need a lawyer." At least she hoped she didn't, Simone thought, pushing past him.

"Get one," he said, moving closer. Too close to her for her peace of mind.

Simone didn't answer. She walked away. Past the ice sculpture area. Past the person in the giant penguin costume. Past the holiday train taking little kids around the zoo. All the while, Gideon remained a step behind her. Was he going to follow her the few blocks home?

Bizarrely, it almost seemed as if they were on a bad date. She couldn't shake the feeling, the absurd sense of connection that didn't exist anymore.

Except for Drew.

Suddenly it occurred to her that if Gideon knew everything else about her life, he might know that he was Drew's biological father, as well.

Fear froze her in front of the plate glass wall where a handful of people watched polar bears frolicking in ice-cold water. She saw Gideon's reflection next to hers in the window and tried to read him.

Did he know? Is that what this interference in her life was about?

When the other spectators drifted away, Simone said, "You've got a lot of nerve, walking back into my life and telling me what to do."

"You're going to fault me because I don't want to see you go to prison for a murder you didn't commit?"

"Feeling guilty, are we?" Her chest squeezed tight. "Thinking of my father and the way you lied on the stand to put him away?"

"I didn't lie and I don't have any reason to feel guilty."

She wanted to believe him…and she wanted to believe her father, as well. Only one of them had been telling the truth during the trial.

And to her.

So if he wasn't feeling guilty…

"Then why?"

"Because I once loved you, Simone."

Her breath left her in a whoosh and her pulse rushed through her so fast the sound filled her ears. She hadn't expected that.

I once loved you…

How could he be saying that when he had betrayed her, making sure her father would rot in prison the rest of his life?

She faced him directly and asked, "Are you sure you don't have some ulterior motive for wanting to help me? Maybe you think I won't tell Michael where to find you."

The way Gideon looked at her made Simone's stomach knot. His expression was a combination of anger, disappointment and something more elusive.

"Would you really sic your brother on me?"

Of course she wouldn't, but Simone didn't say so. Let him think what he wanted of her. Although she knew it was wrong—even though he deserved to sweat—she knew it also gave her a tiny margin of protection from him.

"Just to be perfectly clear," Gideon stepped closer,

crowding her personal space, "I'm not afraid of Michael. I despise what the man represents. I know he can be dangerous, *but so can I.*"

Convinced of that, Simone stepped back again. *Dangerous.* What did he mean?

Had he joined the dark forces that ran things under the civilized veneer of the city? But he'd said he despised what Michael represented…

"You really think you can prove *I'm* innocent?" she asked. "How?"

"By finding the real murderer, Simone."

"What? You're a P.I. on the side when you're not running the club?"

"So to speak. I have connections."

"Connections." She imagined he did. She imagined all kinds of things about this man called Gideon, who'd placed himself right under Michael's nose. "What does that mean? What kind of connections? Who—"

"Interested parties who want to see justice done."

Vigilantes?

Simone thought about it for a moment and decided that the description fit him in an odd way. Years ago, he'd needed someone to pay for his father's murder and he'd picked her father, Frank Ruscetti's rival. He'd done what he'd needed to make "justice" happen.

"Why does it sound like there have been others before me?" Simone asked.

"Because there have been. A few."

"Murder?"

"Remember the Elise Mitchell case?"

"I read about it. The woman was sent to prison for killing her husband. She escaped to protect her child and managed to draw out the real murderer."

"With our help. Her current husband is a detective, an unofficial member of our team. And more recently, an ex-priest named Dermot O'Rourke was framed for murder and we helped clear his name, as well."

"Are your results always this good?"

"Perfect record."

While Simone's curiosity grew, she fought with herself. Not that she was so fond of the justice system, not after her father had been incarcerated for something he said he didn't do. All Gideon's fault. Letting him get too close wouldn't be smart. It wouldn't be good for her or for Drew. Her son had been given no reason to doubt that David was his father. What if Gideon figured out the deception and told Drew the truth?—that David hadn't even been related to him? It would break Drew's heart. She couldn't do that to him.

"If you won't say yes for yourself, do it for your son," he said.

"What?" It was as if Gideon was inside her head and privy to those thoughts. Her heart threatened to pound right out of her chest. Surely he hadn't found out about Drew.

"If you go to jail, what will happen to him?"

"Michael—"

"Yeah, Michael," Gideon said. "Is that what you want?"

"Michael loves Drew—"

"And he'll be happy to corrupt the kid, turn him into an imitation of himself. You know I'm right."

That Gideon *was* right ate at Simone. Michael's influence on Drew was the very thing she feared most. She was caught in a conundrum. She didn't want Gideon's help because it might hurt her son; not taking his help—her landing in prison—might hurt Drew even more.

"All right." Her words were as wooden as her thoughts. Trapped. She was trapped and not even in a jail cell. "Help me clear my name."

And then get out of my life before you ruin it again.

GIDEON HAD generously offered Simone help and then he'd had to convince her to take it. How absurd, he thought.

Why should he care whether or not Simone Burke wanted his help?

Wanted him?

Did she equate the two?

Did he?

As they stopped near the birds of prey exhibit, lights twinkling around Simone made her look like some Christmas fairy dressed in green. It almost hurt physically to look at her angelic face, to remember what they'd once had…what he'd lost…what could have been.

"We need to meet with my people," he said, tersely adding, *"Now."*

Her eyes widened and her mouth turned down in annoyance. "What if I have other plans for the evening?"

"You have something more important going on than ducking a murder charge?"

That deflated her, and then something inside Gideon softened. Suddenly Simone looked vulnerable...like the scared girl he remembered before the trial. Back then, he'd wanted to take her in his arms and tell her how much he loved her, how horrible he felt knowing his father's murder was ripping them apart.

Back then, Michael had stood between them and had kept Simone from the trial, had kept him from seeing Simone ever again.

But Michael wasn't here now.

Gideon reached out and touched her cheek. Though Simone's eyes widened, she didn't move away. Fingertips burning where they met her delicate skin, he slid his hand back around her neck, and tugged her closer. She leaned into him and he wrapped his arms around her back. He held her and wondered how he'd gone without this...this feeling of rightness for so long. He'd never felt with another woman the way he did with Simone in his arms.

He needed objectivity, to be able to stand back and not let Simone get to him. Wanting to do more than just hold her, he, instead, did nothing at all.

The hardest nothing *of his life.*

Simone suddenly came awake, pushing at him with frantic intensity. So she felt it, too, Gideon thought, smiling as he let her go.

"There'll be no more of that," she gasped.

"No more of what?"

"Holding? Comforting?"

"No, I mean yes!"

"Touching?"

"You want your hand broken?"

"I get the picture, Simone." He grinned down at her. "So do you."

"Is your ego inflating again?"

"It's not my ego that I'm worried about inflating," he clarified.

Gideon almost laughed at her outraged expression as she realized what he meant. Fearing that she would go back on her agreement with his offer if he didn't back off fast, he lost the smile and gestured for them to start heading in the direction they had come.

When she stood firm, her jaw set, he said, "The parking lot is that way."

"I know where the parking lot is. I walked here."

"I didn't. And since we're heading for Club Undercover, a vehicle would be in order. Unless you want to break in those designer boots."

Sighing, Simone stalked off toward the parking lot. Gideon was content to follow, admiring his view of her swaying hips.

Fate had pulled them apart. Now it had brought them back together, but Gideon knew it was only temporary. He had to remember that if he wanted to stay sane.

CLUB UNDERCOVER sat on an angled street about a two-mile shot from downtown in the Wicker Park/Bucktown neighborhood, originally known as the Polish Gold

Coast. Things changed, Simone knew. For decades, the neighborhood had seen hard times. Once a haven for artists and students, the area was on its way up. The less affluent were being replaced by high-income residents as the neighborhood became gentrified. Still, for now, the area continued to be an eclectic mix—the purple-haired, tattooed and pierced mingling with those dressed in upscale suits and designer duds.

On a clear night like tonight, the lit skyscrapers in the heart of the city appeared to be close enough to touch. Almost romantic. Simone shook away that thought as Gideon handed off the car to a valet.

Although it was Sunday, the club was so popular that lines had already formed along Milwaukee Avenue. Patrons in their twenties and thirties were somehow having conversations despite the competing thump-thump of bass coming from the sound system below.

Simone was glad Gideon steered her through the crowd and down the stairs and not past the area where Al Cecchi had been murdered.

"Mags, alert everyone that I'll be in my office," Gideon told the hostess, who was wearing low riders, thick-soled boots and a sparkly green backless top, a headset tucked into her short hair spiked with glittery green.

"Got it, boss."

Simone followed Gideon into his office, stark with black and chrome furniture and walls the same deep blue as his eyes. Eyes she avoided meeting. She hated that she felt vulnerable in his presence. Hated that she had to depend on him to get her out of trouble.

Thankfully, they weren't alone for long. Before she knew it, Simone was surrounded by testosterone—Blade Stone, the guy who'd been tending bar in the silent auction area; Gabe Connor, the security chief; John Logan, a detective with the CPD. Then a breeze of fresh air waltzed into the room—Cassandra Freed—and Simone took a calming breath.

"Hang in there," Cass murmured, patting her shoulder before taking a seat.

"We're all here, so we can get started," Gideon said. "Logan, what's the status of the official investigation?"

"Several people are suspects, Simone here still being number one on the list. You picked up the dagger, right?"

Simone started. "Yes, but—"

"Just because you touched it doesn't always mean a print will show," Logan went on. "Or it could be smeared. At any rate, it'll take a while to get the prints through the AFIS—that's the Automated Fingerprint Information System. Days, maybe weeks, and—"

"Wait a minute!" Simone interrupted, glaring at Gideon. "Do you mean to say you already talked this over with your people before I even agreed to take your help?"

"We all have a vote here. *They* had to agree before I could approach you."

"Your priorities are a little skewed," Simone said tersely. She looked around at them. "So why did you all agree?" She zeroed in on Logan. "Especially you. You could lose your standing with the police department if they knew what you were doing."

"That's why we don't advertise," Gideon said.

"I was talking to him. So, why?"

"Cops are only human," Logan said, flicking an invisible piece of lint from his suit jacket. "We follow a trail of bread crumbs and hope it takes us to the right conclusion. Sometimes the bread crumbs are wrong. My wife was set up to take the fall for a killer." His voice softened. "If we didn't help her, she might be dead instead of in bed with me on a cold winter night." His gray eyes were intense and his expression serious under his spiked buzz cut. "Gideon says you didn't do it and that's good enough for me."

"Same here," Blade said.

Gabe shrugged. "Me, too."

"Then it's unanimous," Cass added.

Simone understood why Gideon was willing to put himself out—at least, she thought she did—but she didn't know these people. "What do you expect in return? Unfortunately, I'm a little strapped for cash right now—"

"We don't do it for the money." Cass's smile was brittle as she said, "When you do time for a crime you didn't commit, you can't ever get those years of your life back."

Simone had the vague feeling that this was more personal for Cass than it was for Logan. She looked at each of them, Gabe and Blade included, and noted their serious expressions. Whatever their reasons for helping her, they all seemed sincere.

"So how do we start?"

"We need to take a look at all the suspects," Logan said.

"How many are there?"

Gabe snorted. "How many people had reason to hate a lawyer?"

"Hey!" Blade objected.

"Sorry. Criminal lawyer," Gabe said. "I didn't mean to include Lynn."

Cass explained, "Lynn Cross is a divorce attorney. She and Blade are engaged."

"My husband was a lawyer, too," Simone said. "And a good man."

"Okay, no lawyer comments," Gideon said bluntly. "What about Cecchi?"

Simone shrugged. "I didn't exactly keep up with him and his clients."

"Narrow it down to anyone at the party."

"Nikki Albright." Even as she said the woman's name, Simone felt cold inside. She'd been wrongly accused and didn't want to do the same to anyone else. Not that she was accusing Nikki, she told herself; she was simply investigating possibilities. The justification making her feel better, she said, "Cecchi got Nikki's ex-husband off on charges of sexually assaulting a minor. She thought that ruined her divorce settlement. Nikki wanted a little payback. That's why she was so determined to win Al's desk at auction. Which she did."

"Nikki Albright is on the list," Logan confirmed. "Have you ever known her to be violent?"

Simone shook her head. "Only to be greedy and a

liar. She couldn't have seen me stab Al because I didn't do it."

"She already admitted she didn't see it, that she merely stumbled onto you standing over the body."

"Thank God."

"That doesn't leave you in the clear," Logan said. "Several people heard your argument over money. And a couple of people saw you with that dagger in your hand."

"I picked it up off the floor. Galen O'Neill also handled it. She said she was bidding on it for her husband, but I wonder. I had this odd feeling…as if she wanted it for herself."

Logan nodded. "Apparently, she did win the bid."

"Then shouldn't she be suspect?" Blade asked.

Simone didn't really think the normally timid Galen was capable of violence. But what about self-protection? Hesitantly, she said, "Galen and Al had words earlier in the evening. What if he blamed her for losing his desk and went after her in the corridor?"

"Cecchi was arguing with everyone," Blade said. "Including his wife."

"Neither woman is in the clear," Logan stated. "Anyone else you can think of?" His gaze penetrated Simone.

She shifted in her seat. Only one other person she could think of—Michael. But her brother had promised to stay out of it. As far as she knew, Michael had never set foot in the auction area.

"No one," she said.

"I think we should start with the wife, find out what she knows," Gideon said, his gaze never leaving Simone's face. "See if she's a grieving widow or otherwise."

Grieving widow...

His words got to Simone. Was he questioning her loyalty to David? Or was it her guilt that she still was attracted to Gideon getting to her?

"Right. We can talk to Teresa," she agreed. "Then what?"

"I'll keep you informed if anything new breaks in the investigation," Logan said.

Gabe raised his hand. "If you need any high-tech spy toys, I'm your man."

"I'll be backup wherever," Blade offered. "Bodyguard. If you need me to follow someone..."

Right, a tall muscular man with long hair, a hawklike nose and high cheekbones would really blend in anywhere.

"And I want you to introduce me as a potential member of the Chicago Philanthropic Club."

Simone started at Cass's request. "You really want to be a member?"

Cass nodded. "I may not have a lot of money, but I make up for it in enthusiasm. Besides, I want to get a feel for the other suspects."

"Feel? Are you a closet therapist?"

"She's a closet psychic," Gideon said.

Great. Just when she was beginning to think she could breathe a little easier, they had to go and pull the rug out from under her.

"Gideon's exaggerating," Cass was quick to assure her. "I'm simply more intuitive than they are. It seems like we need to cover all the key players at the charity event to see what they have to say about Al Cecchi. Getting the truth out of people is something I'm good at face-to-face. I just…know things."

"Great," Simone said, aloud this time, trying not to show how shaken up she really was. She plastered a smile on her face. "Let's get started."

Chapter Five

As they drove toward the Central Station neighborhood for a surprise visit to Teresa Cecchi, Simone figured she should have known she was going to be thrown into close contact with Gideon by accepting his help. Had that been why he'd volunteered?

"So what do you think of Cecchi's widow?" Gideon asked.

"Teresa? She's all right. We were never close. She was always pleasant to me, the way wives of business partners usually are to each other."

Simone hated bothering the widow, especially with three children to comfort. She'd heard the wake would be the following night. So what if Teresa had been having problems with Al—she'd been married to him for nearly thirty years. But Gideon had deemed the visit necessary, and the sooner the better. He assured Simone the detectives had already questioned Teresa.

"Do you think Teresa Cecchi could commit murder?" he asked.

Simone's throat tightened. "I think there are a lot of people who could kill someone under extreme circumstances, but I don't want to be the one who decides who could do it and who couldn't."

"I was simply asking for an opinion."

"One I obviously am not comfortable giving."

Which *he* obviously was.

He'd easily testified against her father, as she well remembered. Perhaps he'd had reason to believe Papa had wanted his father dead. Which could have set him up mentally so that he saw what he'd expected to see that fateful night. She found it so difficult to believe that the young man she'd loved had outright lied, but she could believe that he'd been mistaken, that he'd been guilty of bad judgment rather than out-and-out betrayal.

After a moment, Gideon said, "You know, Simone, investigations aren't perfect. They're fact-gathering with a lot of supposition thrown in to get to the next step. Unfortunately, the truth doesn't neatly present itself."

"I'm aware of that, but I thought we were simply going to ask Teresa about any of Al's potential enemies. Anyone who might have threatened him."

"We will. But you have to open your mind to all the possibilities so that you can find the kernels of truth in whatever she tells us. I'm not sure what good any of this is going to do if you won't even try to draw conclusions from what we learn."

"I don't, either. So maybe trying to find the killer is a waste of time."

"We don't have to do this."

Her feeling of being trapped intensified. "I only wish that were true."

Simone was glad to sink into silence as they turned off State Street. They wound through a newly developed neighborhood of condos, town houses and single family homes, which sat west of the Museum Campus, the grassy knoll along Lake Michigan with walking paths, sculptures and flower beds connecting the Field Museum to the Shedd Aquarium and Adler Planetarium.

They approached the Museum Vista development where Simone pointed to a three-story single-family home of brown brick and gray stone. "It's that one."

Gideon whistled. "A minimansion."

"It's a lot of house," Simone agreed. "Especially since only one son visits from college and stays here a few weeks out of the year. The other two children live on their own. I wonder if all the rooms have ever been used for anything more than a few parties." That was the only reason she'd been inside.

"It sounded as if Cecchi was in the doghouse, so probably two of those bedrooms were in use," Gideon mused as he parked the car. "The question is, did his wife want him removed from her bed permanently?"

Though it was after nine when they rang the bell, a fiftyish woman dressed in a starched-looking, conservative dark gray dress answered the door. A new employee, Simone thought, remembering the former maid had been younger and prettier. Considering the hour, the maid was no doubt a live-in.

"Mrs. Cecchi isn't expecting anyone tonight," the woman announced.

Simone gave her a practiced smile. "I'm aware that she's in mourning, but would you please tell her that Simone Burke is here?"

Thick brows furrowed over narrow dark eyes. "I'm sorry, the mistress is not receiving guests."

"I'm not exactly a guest."

"Mrs. Cecchi and Ms. Burke are business partners," Gideon clarified, his low tone vibrating along Simone's skin. "The matter is urgent."

"Well, I shall see what I can do. You may wait in the foyer," the woman said, stepping back to let them in.

The foyer was nearly as large as Simone's living room. The floor was pale yellow marble, and the walls were lined in yellow silk. There were two chairs with a narrow table to one side of the door, but Simone preferred to stand.

The moment the maid disappeared through a doorway that led to the back of the house, Simone murmured, "Business partners?"

"Both law partners are dead, so the business belongs to the surviving spouses. Right?"

"I hadn't thought of it that way, considering neither of us is a lawyer."

"The clients are among the potential assets. You need to start thinking about protecting your investments."

But with Al dead, Simone could see all the law firm profits slipping through her fingers for good. She feared losing the money from David's insurance policy, as well.

A moment later, the maid summoned them to follow her to the back of the house. Gideon placed a hand at the small of her back. The warmth of each long finger made a lasting impression. Simone forced herself to walk naturally so she didn't let on that he affected her so much after all these years. After all that stood between them.

Ensconced in her conservatory off the kitchen and family room, Teresa Cecchi didn't look much like the grieving widow. If she was in mourning, Simone couldn't tell. No grief-stricken family members surrounded her. Her face wasn't swamped with tears. Her eyes weren't even swollen and red. In fact, Teresa was busy tending to a large, blooming Christmas cactus. Teresa hummed to herself as she worked over the sink, spraying the plant—resplendent with blooming flowers that matched the fiery red of her sweater—with a fine mist.

"You have my condolences, Teresa," Simone said, feeling a bit better about intruding. "I'm very sorry about Al." When the woman didn't answer, she gave Gideon a puzzled look and murmured, "Beautiful plant."

"Don't get any ideas, Simone," Teresa said without looking up. "The plant is mine."

"Yes. Of course it is."

"As is everything you see here. The house. The furnishings. *Everything*."

Thinking the new widow must be grieving in her own way, and therefore not in her right mind, Simone fell silent. Teresa set down the hose, picked up a set of hand shears and started trimming back the plant. She eyed Gideon between snips.

"And who might this be?"

He started, "The name's Gideon—"

"Your new lover, Simone?" Teresa asked, cutting him off. "My, you are a fast worker, I'll give you that."

Simone was speechless for the moment.

"You flatter me," Gideon said, but Teresa wasn't being charmed.

"Slut!" the woman said vehemently.

"E-excuse me?"

"There is no excuse for your poor taste, Simone. David is only dead what? Six months?"

A strangled "Eight" came out of Simone. Was her attraction to Gideon so very apparent?

"And already you're on your second replacement."

"Second?" Gideon murmured.

Confused, Simone said, "Look, Teresa, I don't know what you're implying—"

"You think I'm deaf, dumb and blind? I know what was going on between you and my Albert."

Remembering that Al had said Teresa was delusional, that his wife had thought he was having an affair, Simone protested, "*Nothing* was going on. At least not with me!"

"I know about all those long lunches."

"*Business* lunches. We were talking about money."

"I'll just bet you were," Teresa said, stepping out from her work table, shears still in hand. "How much did Albert give you? Were you worth it?"

Simone gasped. "If you're implying Al and I were intimate, you're mistaken—"

"I know my Albert was irresistible."

"Trust me, I could resist him." She hadn't even liked him. "I loved David and still mourn him." She was aware of Gideon shifting beside her as if he were suddenly uncomfortable.

"I know your type," Teresa continued. "You can't be without a man, so you went after my husband."

"You couldn't be more wrong. I was simply trying to get Al to turn over David's share of the profits so I could support my son."

"A likely story!"

"The truth! Look, Teresa, don't let your imagination run away with you. All I was looking for was money that David brought in—"

"You won't be getting anything from me!"

Teresa was waving the sharp shears wildly now, and Simone thought the little woman was dangerous. She stepped back and smacked into Gideon, who put hands on her shoulders to steady her.

"I think you need to put down the shears," Gideon said. "You might hurt yourself."

A threatening expression wreathed Teresa's face as she glared at Simone, but eventually, she set the shears down on the workbench.

"You've given me your condolences," the widow said, her voice stiff. "Fine. So if that is all, I shall have Hannah see you to the door."

"It isn't all," Gideon said. "We need to talk about who might possibly have killed your husband."

"How do I know *she* didn't? Besides, Albert's death is none of your business!"

"You're mistaken. I own Club Undercover where he was murdered."

Teresa shrugged indifferently. "I've already spoken to the authorities."

"We were hoping you would speak to us, as well," Simone said.

"Why should I?"

"You want your husband's murderer caught, right?" Gideon asked.

Simone watched Teresa carefully, but the widow's face was expressionless.

"Of course," she finally said, turning her gaze to Simone once more. "Albert was *my* husband."

"And *I* didn't have an affair with him or kill him, no matter what Nikki Albright said. So please, Teresa, talk to us."

The widow seemed to think it over. Simone could tell she wanted them out of her home, but something stopped her from insisting.

"All right." Teresa marched over to a side door and opened it. "In here. I need a drink."

By the time Simone and Gideon had followed her into a small den—consisting of a fireplace, book-lined walls, a leather love seat and chair and a couple of small tables—Teresa Cecchi already had a drink in her hand. Without offering one to Simone or Gideon, she crossed to the chair, leaving the love seat for them. Hoping that Gideon would stand, Simone sat gingerly to one side, but he immediately took the other, crowding her with his closeness.

"So what is it you think I can tell you?" Teresa asked.

"The obvious," Gideon stated. "Did your husband have any enemies? Anyone you might have forgotten to mention to the police?"

"He was a criminal lawyer who represented the scum of the earth. What do you think?"

"Anyone who actually threatened him?"

"You mean seriously? Not that I'm aware of. Then, again, Albert was good at keeping things from me," Teresa muttered, downing half of her drink in one gulp.

"That's why you put his desk up for auction."

"Exactly. The worm deserved to suffer." Teresa sideswiped Simone with an accusatory stare.

"Again, if he was having an affair, it wasn't with me." Simone wondered if the woman really was insane. "How can you be so sure Al was unfaithful?"

"Oh, please, give me some credit, Simone. A man doesn't make late night calls for no reason."

"They could have been calls to a client."

"More than once when he realized I was nearby, he hung up fast."

"That's it?"

"He'd been staying out late, telling me he was working, but he wasn't at the office. I checked. Then there was the money. It was disappearing from our accounts on a regular basis, but not to pay our bills. And of course, the perfume on his jacket wasn't something he was buying for me. I've always preferred a light floral scent, and this was heavy and exotic. And it wasn't the first time he wore her stink home," Teresa said, her distaste obvious. "But it was the last."

Finally, a crack in Teresa's armor. Her eyes appeared watery and she seemed to be making a great effort to keep herself under control.

"That's it." Teresa abruptly got to her feet. "You'll both have to leave now."

Simone sensed Teresa's patience was at an end, no doubt because she'd let her emotions show for a moment. "Thank you, Teresa. If you think of anything else…"

"I'll certainly inform the police."

Hannah appeared out of nowhere and escorted them to the front door, sliding a dead bolt into place behind them.

They were barely down the steps when, sarcasm rich in his voice, Gideon said, "That went well."

"Right. We know exactly what we knew before going to see her."

"Not exactly."

"What do you mean?" she asked, as Gideon opened the passenger door for her.

"She doesn't seem to be the grieving widow."

"I disagree."

Teresa had put up an I-don't-care-because-he-betrayed-me front, but there'd been that one moment when the other woman had opened herself to feelings deeper than anger. Simone saw Teresa as a woman who was trying to hide the fact that she still loved her faithless—and now dead—husband.

The phrase *crime of passion* came to mind—perhaps Teresa killed Al out of jealousy—but she brushed it aside.

As they pulled away from the curb and headed for the main street, she said, "I mean, I would have agreed with you first—Teresa didn't seem properly distraught—but she was off guard there at the end."

"I didn't notice."

Thinking of how she'd reacted when David had died, Simone said, "Perhaps you've never really grieved for the loss of someone you loved," before remembering his father had been murdered.

Gideon's hands tightened on the steering wheel, but he didn't comment. Simone shifted uncomfortably in her seat anyway.

He turned at the corner, saying, "Maybe the widow Cecchi was trying to cover up the fact that she killed her husband. She was really angry with him. She was angry with *you* tonight, thinking you were Cecchi's mistress. Are you going to tell me you didn't feel threatened when she wielded those shears in your direction?"

"Only for a moment."

"A moment is all it takes to kill someone. You never know what one will do in the heat of passion."

Gideon slid a look her way, and Simone suddenly felt uneasy at the mention of passion. She forced herself to concentrate on their investigation.

"There was something else the widow said," Gideon mused. "In defending her mistress theory, she let it slip that money had disappeared and not toward paying their bills."

"Obviously she figured he was lavishing it on this other woman."

"Maybe he was. Maybe that's why he'd been putting you off about making a cash settlement."

"That's an awful lot of money to waste on a mistress."

"Maybe he didn't consider it wasted."

"Or maybe something else was going on."

They fell silent for a moment before Gideon said, "See, you can do it, after all."

"Do what?"

"Speculate. Take things you heard a what-if step closer to the truth."

"Maybe I should become a private investigator."

"A career option."

For a tiny second, Simone wondered what it would take to get licensed before shaking away the silly idea. She needed a job, one she was qualified to do. "What next? How do we find a potential murderer?"

"It might help to get a look at Cecchi's files. If any client threatened him, surely he would have made a note of it. Logan said the detectives are working on a court order to search the office."

"I don't need a court order. I have keys."

"Then let's go. What's the address?"

"I don't have the office key ring on me." Simone checked her watch and realized that Drew would be home by now. "I need some time at my place anyway. But I can meet you later."

"How much later?"

"What are you doing at midnight?"

WHEN SIMONE arrived home in a taxi she didn't expect to see her brother's vehicle parked in front of the house. Tonight of all nights…

Thank goodness she'd refused to let Gideon bring her all the way home. She hadn't wanted a chance meeting between him and Drew, so she'd insisted he let her off at North and Clark, near the zoo. She'd figured he could go straight west to the club from there. She could tell he'd wanted to argue with her, but he'd restrained himself.

A good thing, or he might have run into Michael.

She realized with a start that this was the second time she thought of protecting Gideon from her brother. She was going to have to deal with her unresolved feelings for Gideon sometime. Just not now or anytime soon, she decided, heading down the gangway to the rear of the house and the kitchen entrance.

Circling the back porch, she noted a bulky silhouette leaning against a rail. "Ulf," she murmured, acknowledging Michael's bodyguard.

Blond hair fell over his pale eyes as he bobbed his head toward her. "Ma'am."

Simone sighed. *Ma'am* was right up there with *maven*. Not that she was obsessed with perpetual youth, but she was far from middle-aged and was beginning to wonder if worry was taking its harsh toll on her.

"Don't you ever get tired of waiting on my brother."

"It beats a lot of jobs," Ulf said. "And I don't intend to do it forever."

"Of course you don't."

But he probably would. Michael's employees seemed to be inexplicably tied to him. He'd once laughingly said that when he hired someone, it was "until death do us part." Unfortunately, Simone didn't think he'd been joking.

When Ulf opened the kitchen door for her, male laughter spilled out into the night. Simone smiled, pleased that her son was laughing again.

"Hey, did someone tell a good joke?"

"I did," Michael said, "but it's a guy thing."

"A guy thing, huh?"

Sighing, she looked from the nearly empty pizza box sitting on the coffee table to her son.

Drew wasn't smiling.

"Why didn't you tell me, Mom?" he demanded.

"Tell you what?" Simone tensed at her son's serious expression.

"That Al Cecchi was murdered last night and you might be arrested for murdering him. I'm not a kid anymore," he said in a sullen tone. "Why were you trying to hide that from me?"

"Have some respect for your mother," Michael admonished him. "She didn't kill anyone."

"Some people think she did."

"What people?" Simone asked, wondering if her own son could be one of them. Drew looked angry. Her stomach knotted with guilt. "Is my name in the papers?"

"No," Michael assured her. "That would spell a lawsuit. You haven't been arrested."

Yet, Simone thought.

"The word's going around, Mom. My friends all know Nikki Albright thinks you did it. Why would she accuse you?"

"I don't know!" Simone snapped, upset enough to cry. "Maybe she's trying to cover up for herself?" The words were out of her mouth before she realized what she was saying. She hadn't meant to accuse anyone else of the crime.

Simone checked her watch. "It's getting late."

Drew stared at her with slitted eyes, the same way Gideon used to. The resemblance took her breath away.

"Sorry, Uncle Mike," he said, "but I get up at the crack of dawn for work tomorrow."

"You don't have to do that, you know." Michael threw an arm around the teenager's shoulders and squeezed affectionately. "I can get you a cushy job—"

"Michael!" Simone glared at her brother.

"It's okay, Uncle Mike. I like my job."

"If you change your mind…"

Drew gave him a crooked grin and took the stairs two at a time. He didn't so much as look back at her.

Taking a deep breath to ease the knot in her middle, Simone said, "I wish you wouldn't do that."

"Do what? Bring pizza? It's good. Try it."

"You're not going to distract me. Drew has good values, and I would like to see him keep them."

Michael's visage darkened. "You're saying I have bad values?"

For a moment, Simone couldn't look at her brother. He knew how she felt about his business, no matter that he'd reassured her he'd gone straight when he took over from Papa. For a moment, she thought about bringing the subject into the open again. But they'd lived so long not talking directly about what he did for a living.

Michael had protected and taken care of her ever since they had been kids. And he'd been so good to her, Drew and David. She loved him unconditionally, and she didn't want to put an end to their relationship. And so once more she danced around the truth.

"Offering your nephew a cushy job so he doesn't have to work hard? Yes, I would say that's not what I want my son to learn from you."

"All right. I get the picture. You and David never would let me spoil my nephew."

"He's a good kid, Michael. I want him to stay that way. I don't want him taking the easy way."

"About last night," he said, suddenly changing the subject. "Sorry I wasn't there to help you out."

Part of Simone was sorry, the other part glad. If her brother had stuck around, for sure he and Gideon would have come face-to-face.

"What happened to you, anyway?"

Michael grinned. "I met someone…um…interesting."

"Bared midriff, purple-streaked hair?"

"That would be the one. The party wasn't really her kind of scene. Not mine, either. So we took it elsewhere." His smile suddenly faded. "Good thing we weren't at the club or I would've had the police breathing down my neck just for being there. *You* weren't thinking I had anything to do with Cecchi's murder?"

Simone tried to cover the guilt she felt for initially suspecting Michael. "I was just wondering where you were, is all. I guess it's a good thing you weren't there."

"So you didn't tell anyone that I'd offered to take care of Cecchi for you?"

"Of course not."

Still appearing unsettled, Michael nodded. "Trouble never leaves us DeNalis alone."

Simone didn't want her son getting into trouble. Some would say that was the fate of a DeNali, even if he carried a different last name. But she was determined to do whatever it took to keep Drew safe.

How, when she herself might be in hot water? an internal voice taunted.

What if determination wasn't enough?

"SO WHAT IS IT between you and Simone?" Cass asked Gideon when she caught him at the upstairs bar nursing a shot of hundred-dollar-a-bottle tequila. "The problem, I mean."

Gideon let the liquor roll over his tongue and down his throat. "Who said there was a problem?"

When Cass raised her eyebrows and stared at the glass in his hand, Gideon grunted. Of course Cass knew, even if she didn't know the specifics.

"It was a long time ago."

He finished the shot and signaled Blade for another, silently willing Cass to take the hint and do a disappearing act. The club was in full swing, couples dancing in each others arms on the floor below to a slow tune that dripped with sensuality and made him think of Simone.

"First love?" Cass asked, leaning in close and keeping her voice low.

"Why the interest?"

"Because I care about you, Gideon, and I want to see you happy. You're lonely and—"

He barked a laugh. "How could I be lonely running this club, and with a certain person choosing to stick her nose in my business."

"But you have no one to go home to at night."

"Neither do you."

Cass shrugged. "We're not talking about me. Whatever it is that Simone did to you, it didn't change the way she felt about you."

"You can't know that…can you?"

"I don't have to be psychic to know it. I just have to see her eyes when she looks at you. They're filled with longing and a great sadness. Just as your eyes are when you look at her."

Blade set another drink before him but didn't linger. Too busy filling orders.

"Some things were just not meant to be," Gideon said.

"Maybe. But how do you know this was one of those things? Simone walked back into your life in a very dramatic way…like maybe you were supposed to pay attention. And you have, at least on the surface by agreeing to help clear her. That gives you both a chance to see what you missed. I believe in second chances, Gideon, and I know you do, as well, or Team Undercover wouldn't exist. Since I've known you, giving others a second chance has been your reason for being. So why don't you give one to yourself?"

A second chance...

Gideon thought about it as he finished his drink. Alone. Cass was right. He was always alone. Even in the midst of a crowd like tonight. Bodies and noise and hard work—none of those things could fill up the empty space inside.

He hadn't always felt empty.

There'd been the time before the running, when all the world had been ahead of him and Simone...

But what if she'd known that her father meant to kill his? he asked himself for the millionth time. If only he knew what she'd meant to tell him that night.

What would it be like, he wondered, if he could forget the past, if he could have Simone in his life again, not as a client—a victim who needed his help—but as a woman who needed him as a man?

Gideon set down his glass and considered finding out.

Chapter Six

By the time Simone arrived downtown, Gideon was waiting for her. As she walked from her car, she spotted him at the front doors of the building housing her late husband's law offices. Gideon seemed so sure of himself, so in control, that her heart quickened a beat.

But when the first words out of his mouth were "You're late"—not exactly a friendly greeting—she stopped short and adjusted her attitude.

"I had an unexpected delay." She hesitated a moment before adding, "Michael stopped by."

"Out of the blue, huh? And right after one of his lawyers gets killed."

Simone started. "Al Cecchi wasn't Michael's lawyer." He hadn't been in years.

"He was with LaFuria and Mazzoni, who represented your father. When did that change?"

The reminder of the trial and *his* part in it made Simone's stomach clench. "Not long after Papa went to prison, Al left the firm to open his own office."

"With your late husband."

She nodded. "Michael didn't come with them." At her insistence. Not wanting to be distracted by the reminder of their tangled past, she asked, "Can we go in now? It's cold out here."

"Let me help you with that."

Before she could protest, he slipped an arm around her shoulders. Ignoring the sudden flush of warmth shooting through her, Simone headed for the outside doors and used her coded key card to unlock them. She had to stop this…this unreasonable response she had to the man. There'd been nothing personal in her agreeing to let him help her. He owed her family, she thought resentfully.

"No security here at night?" Gideon suddenly asked.

"There's security 24/7," Simone assured him. "Just not a doorman after hours."

She had no idea if the watchman was pacing the corridors the way he was supposed to be or if he was ensconced in some office talking on the phone with his girlfriend or surfing the TV.

Besides, she had a right to enter her late husband's offices. The business belonged to her and Teresa now. She wasn't breaking in. Still, she couldn't help but feel ill at ease at their clandestine search.

The office building was old, a thirty-plus-story highrise of the early twenties. The lobby had been restored to its art deco glory—cubic forms, geometric ornamentation and sleek black and green surface materials. Marble floors shone, as did the brass doors of the elevators as they slid open when Simone pressed the Call button.

She hurried inside, away from Gideon, but he managed to crowd her all the way up to the tenth floor. Was he doing it on purpose? she wondered. To make her nervous? Or was he oblivious to the effect he was having on her?

Glancing at Gideon's neutral expression before exiting the elevator car, Simone suspected the latter. He barely seemed to recognize her presence. She dug in her pocket for the key ring that had belonged to David and found the one to the outside office door, which opened easily.

"I'm surprised that Cecchi didn't change the locks when he became sole partner," Gideon said.

"Something he wasn't legally entitled to do until our business was settled."

"Are you saying Al Cecchi worked on the up-and-up?"

"I certainly hope so."

"Then why was he murdered?"

"Isn't that why we're here—to find out?"

At least, that's why she was there, Simone told herself. The only reason she was spending time in Gideon's company.

Though some people might have reason to hate Al, she hadn't considered he might have involved the firm in something illegal. Having come from a connected family himself, David had known that had been a condition of their marriage. He'd told her all that he'd needed to walk the straight and narrow for the rest of his life was a good woman to love. *Her.* Even though he'd had to represent criminals in his work, he'd promised he wouldn't get involved in anything illegal.

But Al had made no such promise.

Gazing around the outer office with its receptionist's desk and seating area, she didn't think anything of importance would be kept out here. But the firm's space was bigger than it initially appeared to be—two windowed offices for the partners, three interior offices for the two associates, a paralegal, three secretaries and an office manager, a conference room, a file room and a supply/copy room.

"Where do we start?" she murmured.

"How about Cecchi's inner sanctum," Gideon suggested.

"Of course."

But the door was locked.

Simone tried various keys on the ring, but none of them turned.

"Open sesame!" she muttered.

"I think that only works in folktales," Gideon said, stepping closer. She immediately backed off. He arched a dark eyebrow at her. "Let me."

"Be my guest."

She held out the key ring, which he ignored.

Simone watched as Gideon slipped a hand beneath his coat and pulled out a small leather case from an inner pocket. She shifted uneasily as he unzipped the case and removed a tension wrench and a lock pick—a long, thin piece of metal that curved up at the end.

"You know how to use those?" Simone whispered as he inserted the tension wrench into the keyhole.

Rather than answer, Gideon inserted the pick into the

keyhole and began manipulating it. The pins of the tumbler softly clicked against the quiet of the night as he lifted them one at a time.

Simone remembered Michael showing her how to pick a lock. He'd told her she would have to learn exactly the right pressure to apply and what sounds to listen for. She'd never been able to perfect her sense of touch to feel the slight movements of pins and plugs or to visualize all the pieces inside as they were manipulated.

She'd been a kid then and had thought it was a fun game. But not now. This was serious business.

Another turn of the tension wrench and the lock gave.

"Open sesame," Gideon said, swinging open the door for her.

Again that vague guilt whispered through her, but Simone ignored it and shut off the lights in the main reception area. In case the security guard came by, she didn't want anything to draw his attention to their presence.

She'd been in Al's office a few times, but tonight nothing seemed familiar. Not the contemporary designer furniture so at odds with the treasured antique desk that had belonged to his mother. Not the Oriental carpet or the paintings that must have cost a small fortune. Not the contrasting modern electronics set out on his desk and in a wall unit behind it.

Had she really been in this room before? Simone wondered, her brow furrowed as she gazed around. Or had Al totally refurbished the place, using David's share of the business to do so?

"Somehow, I wouldn't have guessed this was his style," Gideon said.

"Surprise," she murmured, opening the door to an interior room that held nothing but file cabinets. *So many drawers, so little time.* "So how long do you think it will take us to go through his records?"

She turned to find Gideon at Al's desk, checking his calendar. He picked up a pen and started scribbling something on a pad of paper.

"What are you doing?" she asked.

"Making a list of the clients he's seen or represented in court in the last month. We can check their files and see if we can eliminate some of the names. Then I'll give the remainder to Gabe. He'll run a security check on them."

"It's a place to start, I suppose."

"You don't sound enthusiastic."

"We're invading the privacy of a lot of people."

"You don't think the police will do a thorough search? A man is dead, Simone. Murdered," he reminded her, "and you're still the chief suspect."

Simone couldn't fight his logic.

So she helped Gideon pull files of the people who'd recently met with Al. They eliminated any with charges that were misdemeanors or any of the cases that had been settled in the client's favor.

That left thirty-odd files.

"You go through those, see what you can turn up,"

Gideon said, sitting down before the computer. "I'll see what I can find here."

Simone split the files, sorting them into the cases already settled, pending cases and new cases. She was busy with the last pile, trying to eliminate a few more files, when Gideon's low curse caught her attention.

"Find something?"

"Can't get in. He's password protected."

"Al was pretty much a linear thinker. Try Albert."

"Nope."

"Cecchi."

"Uh-uh."

"Teresa."

"Nada."

Rising, Simone began feeding him the names of Al's kids, but none of those worked, either.

"His initials—AC."

"No."

"*Sicilian Breeze*. Make that one word."

Gideon frowned at her. "You're playing with me now."

"You would know if I was playing. I'm dead serious. It's what he named the yacht he bought last spring, right before David died."

"Yacht, huh?" he muttered, typing in the name. "Big-ticket item."

"No kidding."

"The house…the yacht…this office…" Gideon hesitated a few seconds, then said, "Bingo, I'm in!" For a moment, the office was silent but for the noise his fingers made tapping over the keyboard. Then he said, "Have you considered Cecchi's holdings seem to exceed his half of the partnership? Either that or the firm was worth a whole lot more than you guessed. Of course, his murder will put a whole new edge to your fighting for what's yours."

Something she hadn't thought of. "Another reason to figure out who did it."

Simone attacked the paper files with determination while Gideon hunched over the keyboard. Every so often, she heard him say *hmm* or *huh*. His muttered musings finally got the better of her curiosity.

"What?"

"I got into the accounting records."

"And?"

"You're broke."

"What? You mean Al *did* spend David's share of the business on his lifestyle?"

"He spent it on something. Big withdrawals every couple of weeks."

Simone left her stack of files to come stand behind Gideon and peer at the computer screen. Not that she could make sense of the numbers she was seeing.

"In English," she said.

"I paged down through the accounts until I reached partner withdrawals," Gideon explained. "In every partnership, when a partner takes out cash, it's booked as a reduction in cash and an increase in partner distributions."

"But David has been dead for eight months."

"Doesn't matter. Cecchi's withdrawals still had to be posted like that until he bought you out and closed the books. Only he took so much out of the business, there wasn't enough left to buy you out."

"That bastard!" Simone cried. "All this time he's been putting me off, he's been cashing in. How long has this been going on?"

"For quite a while."

Gideon tapped some keys so that the screen blinked and changed, but it all went by so fast that Simone hardly had time to focus on a column before it changed.

"I'm going backward in time," Gideon explained, "and the withdrawals are getting less obvious." A few more screen changes and he stopped. "It looks like it started last March."

"Two months before my husband died. Surely David would have noticed."

"Maybe. If he was paying attention."

"He never said anything."

"Maybe he didn't want to worry you. Or maybe Cecchi talked to him about it and got your husband's approval. Like I said, the withdrawals were less obvious to start—smaller and farther apart. He could have picked up an expensive habit that snowballed. You might not be able to answer this, but was Cecchi into recreational drugs?"

"Not that I know of. At least, I never saw him using, and David never said anything."

"Maybe another vice?"

"Like a woman," Simone said, deciding that Teresa probably wasn't delusional, after all.

"I'll print out a report and see what else I can find on his computer."

Simone nodded and got back to checking the paper files. After going through them carefully, she kept several to the side. A few cases Al had lost—only one of the offenders was out on the street—a couple in progress that weren't going well, and one new case, only because the name Anthony Viglio was familiar. No doubt David must have mentioned the name. Still, she decided to look at it in more depth.

"I'm going to go in the back room to make some copies to take with us so no one gets suspicious of missing files," she said, thinking of the murder investigation. She didn't want to look any more suspicious in the eyes of the authorities than she already did.

"Good. I'll be done soon," Gideon said. "I'm not finding anything else of interest. But I want to go through Cecchi's desk before we leave."

Simone passed the office that used to be David's. It was empty now of any trace of him, she knew. A few months before, she'd removed all his personal effects. One of the secretaries had already taken care of anything that had to do with the business. Now it was merely a shell of an office. Even so, she stopped for a moment and thought of David before going on.

The small workroom in back was exactly as she'd remembered it. Two walls were lined with supply shelves. The only other objects in the room were a copier and a long table for stacking and sorting.

Simone turned on the copier and got to work. It took

only few minutes to get what she needed. Gathering the original folders and the handful of notes she'd copied from them, Simone switched off the light and returned to Al's office where Gideon was rummaging through the top desk drawer.

She put away the files and stuffed the copied documents into her shoulder bag, then noticed that Gideon had stopped his search to examine what looked like a used party napkin. "What do you have there?"

"A telephone number. No name, though." Gideon pocketed the napkin.

"You're kidding. You're keeping it?"

"Cecchi kept it for some reason. It won't take much to match a name to the number."

"Whatever—"

Simone didn't get a chance to say more, for Gideon had covered her mouth with his hand. Before she could gather her wits, he shoved her away from the desk and against the wall near the door. He put a finger to his lips and then reached across her to switch off the room light.

Pushing at him—Gideon was far too close for her comfort—Simone heard the soft scrape of a lock coming from the other room and realized why he'd pinned her.

She froze.

The outer door…someone else was entering the office.

Her heart beat so fast she swore she could feel it bump against her ribs. Whether it was from the possibility of running into someone dangerous or being so close to Gideon—also, potentially dangerous—she wasn't certain.

Maybe it was just the guard, Simone told herself, trying to keep from trembling. If so, how the heck was she supposed to explain their furtive actions?

Great. Then the security guard would report their presence to the authorities…

She closed her eyes and concentrated on not making a sound. Gideon was still pressed against her, his breath ruffling her hair, reminding her of a night long, long ago. The night Drew was conceived.

Swallowing hard, she filed the memory away and opened her eyes.

Furtive footfalls in the next room and the lack of light told her this wasn't the security guard. Whoever was in the reception area was working in the dark because he didn't want to be seen. A clunk followed by a low curse made Gideon tense against her.

Suddenly a beam of light swept along the wall opposite the open door, and Simone knew the intruder was coming their way. Apparently, so did Gideon. He felt coiled, like a giant spring ready to pop. Simone's throat tightened and breathing became difficult as she waited for the moment when the intruder would zero in on them.

The beam came closer…shone on the open door… swung inward…

Before it swept over them, Gideon lashed out and

Simone gasped, the light danced crazily as it plunged to the floor.

Gideon was in the hallway now. Simone heard feet scuffling. A body bounced off the wall. Simone went after the flashlight that had rolled against the opposite wall. More thumps. Low curses. She wrapped her hand around the flashlight's long metal housing.

The light came up, its beam focused on the reception area. All she saw was a flash of movement before realizing Gideon had stumbled back against a chair. By the time he regained his balance, the intruder was out of the office, slamming the door in Gideon's face.

"Wait!" she whispered, stopping Gideon as he grasped the door handle. "He might have a weapon!"

"If it was a he," Gideon said, not sounding sure. He nodded. "Let's lock up and get out of here before we have the security guard on us, too."

They were out of the office in less than sixty seconds. The corridor was empty. Not having heard the elevator, Simone assumed the intruder had taken the stairs. She didn't realize she was holding her breath until, upon hitting the Call button, the elevator doors opened immediately and she sucked in two lungfuls of air.

Knees rubbery, she hit the button to take them down, then, for the first time, took a good look at Gideon.

His lip was bleeding.

"You're hurt," she murmured, reaching out to touch him.

He caught her wrist and stopped her. "It's nothing."

Maybe she was being ridiculous, but she couldn't

help the little twist she felt inside at the realization that he'd been hurt because of her. And then the twist turned into a falling sensation. The elevator, she thought vaguely. Of course. The elevator was going down.

Though her stomach fluttered and her pulse ticked unevenly, she didn't want to admit it was more than the elevator.

Gideon held her gaze and moved in on her, and Simone fought the panic that filled her. That look in his eyes…she recognized it. Even as a teenager, he'd known what he'd wanted and he'd wanted her.

She'd wanted him in return.

She wanted him now.

At least, part of her did. The other part was shouting *Run!* though there was nowhere to go.

His face inched closer to hers. She trembled. Anticipation warred with dread. One kiss could be deadly, she told herself. She couldn't trust him.

But when his mouth touched hers, the metallic taste of blood sparked something so primal and so deep in her that she moaned into his mouth and parted her lips. It was all the invitation he needed to crush her to him and to invade her mouth as if all their years apart hadn't passed.

As if she were still a teenager dazed by first love.

As if he hadn't betrayed her by taking away her father.

The reminder of what had come between them chilled her inside.

Just as the elevator car came to a stop and the doors opened, Simone twisted out of his arms and ran.

Chapter Seven

Simone ran away from him and out onto the street, just like that last night seventeen years ago, Gideon thought. He followed swiftly but without breaking gait.

She glanced back at him only once before shoving through the outside door. Certain she was going to keep running right out of his life again, he was surprised when she stopped in the middle of the sidewalk.

At her side in no time flat, he gave the surrounding area a once-over for any suspicious characters. Something didn't feel right, yet the only person he saw on the street was a businessman briskly walking to the corner. Apparently the intruder had fled the scene. Still, it wouldn't hurt to stay vigilant.

"You can't run far enough to hide from me," he told Simone, "so you might as well not try."

"I'm not the expert on running, Joey. That would be you." Her tone was as flat as her gaze.

"I'm not Joey Ruscetti any more." He wasn't a kid emotionally crippled by having had his father die in his arms, and so afraid for his mother and sister that, after testifying in court, he'd agreed to leave his home forever. "I'm here to stay, Simone, so get used to it."

Her features remained blank. She'd wrapped herself in a protective frosty air and for the first time he realized how much she'd changed. No mulish expression. No hot words. No true feelings revealed. The girl he'd known was gone, at least for the moment. She'd learned to hide out in the open—no new identity, no new town, but she was hiding from the past every bit as much as he had for seventeen years.

The idea that she'd been forced to learn how to protect herself this way made him angry. This was what being a DeNali had done to the bright, smiling young woman who still lived in his dreams.

Almost forgetting his doubts about Simone—that she might have known her father's plans that fateful night—he said, "I'll see you to your car."

She nodded and started walking. He stayed alongside her, careful not to touch her, and kept his gaze moving, searching the shadows for anything that didn't belong. He couldn't shake the feeling that something was off—that perhaps the intruder was out there, watching. Trusting the instincts that had kept him moving all those years from city to city had been what had kept him alive.

"I need to be at the club early tomorrow, around noon," he said. "If you want to give me the materials you copied, I'll get Gabe right on those security checks."

"Fine."

When she stopped in front of her car, she pulled the copies from her shoulder bag and held them out to him. He was careful that their fingers didn't brush during the transfer.

"So I'll see you tomorrow?" he asked coolly.

"The Chicago Philanthropic Club meets tomorrow morning. Cass is going to be there, too, as she requested. After that. Early afternoon."

"Good."

"Gideon…about the intruder…you said, 'If it was a he.' You think it might have been a woman?"

He shrugged. "It could have been anyone." He didn't really know. "I tried tackling whoever it was, but I couldn't get hold of the person. I felt as if I were grabbing a slippery pillow rather than a solid body."

Simone frowned. "How odd."

No kidding. "You'd better get home and get some rest. You need to be clearheaded tomorrow. On your game. And you want to get home before your kid realizes you're gone, right?"

Simone's eyes widened and her lips parted; something came through that frozen exterior. An emotion he couldn't define slipped out from behind her mask. She looked as if she wanted to say something to him, but then she shifted back into neutral.

"Good night, Gideon."

She slid into the driver's seat. He waited until she'd started the car and pulled away from the curb before he jogged in the other direction to his own vehicle.

The street was deserted and quiet now. Just him and the rumble of a rapid transit train on the elevated structure a block to the west. Still, the hair at the back of his neck bristled. Was it really a warning or was he projecting? But how could he not when someone had broken into the dead man's office while they were in the midst of their own search?

Who was the intruder and what had he—*or she*—been looking for?

The questions were multiplying.

They played through his mind as he drove home and as he sat in the dark, drink in hand, staring out his windows at fresh snow drifting down through the night sky.

BEFORE HE COULD get out of the car, a blue flash froze him to his seat. Another flash. No sound. His father fell into the snow. Still holding his gun in one hand, DeNali lit a cigarette with the other and slid into his vehicle.

Heart pounding, he threw open the door. "Pop!" he yelled, his feet chunking into the drift.

The dark car pulled down the alley.

His eyes flicked to the license plate—RDN 1—before he dropped to the ground next to his father who lay still on his side, a pool of dark blood in the snow before him.

"Pop!" he cried, his voice breaking as he turned his father onto his back. His father had been shot in the gut and the chest. "Can you hear me? Please say you can hear me!"

His father's eyes opened and slowly focused. "Joey…"

"I'll get help, Pop, I'll get someone."

But his father gripped his wrist to stop him. More dark fluid bubbled up from stiff lips.

He rocked his father against him, crying, "What, Pop? What is it?"

"DeNali..."

He continued rocking, knowing it was already too late...

Gideon woke with a start, his heart pounding. Again the dream. Only natural considering how much time he was spending with Simone.

How could he not be reminded of his father's murder?

Rising from the chair, he stared out into the night and wished he could somehow change what happened all those years ago.

"I'M HAPPY to say this year's Red Carpet Christmas cleared a bit over one hundred and fifty-three thousand dollars," Lulu Hutton pronounced on Monday morning as the Chicago Philanthropic Club meeting came to order. "Our most successful fund-raiser ever."

"Successful if you don't count the dead body," a woman sitting near Simone whispered to her friend.

To Simone's horror, the other woman snickered. About to say something, she was stopped by a soothing pat on her arm. She glanced at Cass, sitting next to her. The club's hostess had amazingly transformed herself to blend in with the society women surrounding them. She'd tamed her wild mahogany hair into a twist at the nape of her neck and had donned a conservative dark green suede suit.

Simone smiled at her and tuned out the distasteful exchange so she could concentrate on the president's remarks.

"Here is a breakdown of how the money came in—entries, auction items, donations," Lulu said, distributing a handout. "The second page shows the intended disbursement between the charities we picked for grants."

As usual, the meeting was held over a buffet brunch in a private dining room of a restaurant on the Magnificent Mile. The head of each committee responsible for a grant gave club members an update on her group's specific charity. The report on Umbrella House was left for last since the chairwoman of that committee—Nikki Albright—hadn't shown.

"Still no Nikki?" Lulu said, her smile at war with her annoyed tone.

"Nikki doesn't know the meaning of time," one of the women muttered.

"She'll be late for her own funeral," said another.

The reference made Simone shudder.

Rather than wait any longer, Lulu asked another member of the committee to give an update instead.

After the report, Lulu said, "I'm sure you've all noted we have a guest with us today." She indicated that Cass should stand. "Cassandra Freed, the woman who was responsible for our having Club Undercover for the annual fund-raiser."

A round of applause drew a smile from Cass. "I was happy to do it," she said. "Anything for a good cause."

"Cassandra has applied for membership, so please get to know her a bit better this morning."

As club members gathered in small groups to say hello and the buffet line opened, Simone watched Cass work the room. She was magic. Somehow she managed to engage even the stuffiest of matrons in conversation. Was this the real Cass? Simone wondered. Or simply a great act?

Wondering if Cass was getting any of those vibes she'd mentioned, Simone watched her intently until Galen O'Neill said, "A membership in this club certainly is an unusual choice for someone like her."

Simone didn't let her irritation show. "Yes, giving of one's time is more difficult when one needs to work for a living."

"I meant she's not our sort," Galen went on, apparently not getting Simone's meaning. "What could she possibly have in common with anyone here?"

"The desire to do good?" Simone suggested, wondering about Galen's motivation.

The woman's smile grew tight and again Simone thought there was perhaps more to her than met the eye.

"You don't seem your usual self today," Galen said. "But I imagine you must be a wreck, what with the authorities breathing down your neck about poor Albert's murder. Too bad you picked up that dagger and got your fingerprints all over it."

Simone didn't think Galen sounded at all sympathetic. "I'm sure they'll find the fingerprints of anyone who touched it that night."

Galen blanched and moved on, leaving Simone again wondering if the auction chairwoman had hidden depths.

Galen wasn't the only one interested in the murder. Several other women spoke to her, supposedly to commiserate, but Simone was sure they were simply looking for something juicy to pass on.

"Your attention, please," Lulu said as soon as everyone was seated. "I hope each and every one of you will show your sympathy and support to Teresa Cecchi, who, of course is in mourning and couldn't be with us today. The club is sending a lovely bouquet of flowers for her husband's wake, which will be held the next two evenings, with the church service and a funeral the following morning."

As the club president read off the names and addresses of funeral parlor, church and cemetery, Simone looked around for reactions, but didn't note anyone looking particularly guilty. Though she would rather be anyplace other than at an event honoring the man who'd stolen the money she and Drew should have had, when another member asked if she would be at the wake, Simone knew the smart thing to say was, "Of course. Teresa needs all the support she can get from us."

Whether or not she could carry through with that promise was another matter.

The end of the meeting couldn't come soon enough for Simone. She and Cass were in a taxi on the way to the club before Simone asked Cass if she'd picked up anything interesting.

"Mostly that Al Cecchi wasn't Mr. Popular."

"You didn't get vibes off anyone?"

"From one person," Cass admitted. "The auction chairwoman, Galen O'Neill."

Simone could believe it. Galen hadn't liked Cass being there. "Don't let Galen get to you—"

"She doesn't. I'm not talking about the negative energy she was sending my way. It was something darker."

"I felt that the night of the party," Simone admitted. "Like there was more to her than met the eye."

Cass nodded. "When the announcement about the wake and funeral was being made, I sensed intense emotions—I simply couldn't define them."

"Maybe she was remembering him threatening her."

"Maybe." But Cass didn't sound as if she believed that. "To tell you the truth, I was hoping for more."

"Maybe if Nikki Albright had shown…"

"The woman who accused you?"

"That would be the one." Simone still wondered about Nikki's running into the club hallway so conveniently to accuse *her* of murder.

Cass asked, "So how do I get an introduction?"

Simone realized they weren't far from Nikki's town house. "How about I get you one. Right now."

"Maybe you ought to call first."

"No need. Her place is just ahead in River North—it's on our way."

A few minutes later, they got out of a taxi directly across from Nikki's building. Her unit was at the end of the block of attached brick and greystone row houses. There were no trees or grass, and living quarters were stuck right at the edge of the downtown area. Yet three kids of different ages—siblings from the looks of them—were throwing snowballs at each other on the sidewalk in front.

Too close to the busy street, Simone thought, motherly instincts kicking in as she and Cass passed them and took the steps up to the high stoop.

Nikki didn't answer her bell.

"Looks like she's not home," Cass said.

"Or she's avoiding." Irritated, Simone opened the storm door to knock on the entry door itself, but when her knuckles hit the wooden panel, it creaked inward.

"What the…" Simone met Cass's gaze, which had gone wide-eyed. "Nikki!"

No answering shout.

Uneasy, Simone pushed the door open a bit wider for a view of the foyer and noticed mail strewn on the floor. A small thing to be amiss, yet her heart skipped a beat.

"What now?" Cass murmured.

Probably the smart thing to do would be to turn around and go away. Pretend they had never been here. But what if something was wrong? What if Nikki needed help?

Taking a deep breath, Simone said, "We go in."

"That's called breaking and entering."

"No, not technically. Not the breaking part, anyway. The door is unlocked."

"But we don't have a concrete reason to believe that anything is actually wrong," Cass argued. "Or a reason to be here, for that matter."

How could they just leave without knowing that Nikki was all right?

Simone got creative. "How about…I want to make sure the desk got here safely."

"So you're just going to walk in?"

"Do you want to call the police?" The thought made her stomach knot.

Cass shook her head.

Knowing they could put themselves through hell with the authorities for nothing, Simone said, "Neither do I."

Sensing Cass really didn't want to do this, she remembered the hostess's stance about why Team Undercover was willing to help her—saying something about doing time for a crime not committed.

Maybe Cass had.

"Why don't you wait here, then? I'll just be a minute."

"Simone, this isn't a good idea."

Of course it wasn't, but…

Meaning to reassure Cass, she lost the words when she took a good look at the other woman—pale, distressed.

"What?" Simone demanded.

"I—I'm not sure, but something's really not right."

"You think I'm in danger?"

Cass frowned. "No, not you."

If Cass was having some kind of psychic experience, she certainly wasn't being specific. Simone was torn, but the idea that another human being might need help won out.

"Look, I'll just be a minute. You have your cell phone, right? If you hear or see anything weird, call 911."

Nodding, Cass pulled out her cell.

And Simone cautiously entered the house, again calling, "Nikki!"

She got as far as the entrance to the living room when she froze. The place had been trashed. Couch cushions had been thrown around, chairs upended, books forced from their cases, video and audio equipment out of its media cabinet, drawers pulled out of a wall unit.

But it was the still form in the midst of the chaos that got her complete attention.

"Cass, call 911 now!" she shouted, rushing forward to check for any signs of life.

She'd found Nikki Albright...

Only too late.

Chapter Eight

"So you just happened to be the one who accidentally stumbled over two bodies in three days," Detective Mike Norelli mused as he put the heat on Simone. "Are you sure you wanna stick with that story?"

Middle-aged and beefy, Norelli wore a nondescript dark suit, a white shirt and a forced smile as he questioned her. He hadn't been the detective who'd taken her story at the club—that murder was under investigation by a different area office of the Chicago Police Department. Even so, by the time he'd arrived at Nikki Albright's town house, Norelli had known all about Al Cecchi's murder and that Simone was the chief suspect in that case.

"It's not a story," Simone insisted. "It's the truth. Simple bad luck."

Sitting at the dead woman's dining room table— able to see the investigative team around Nikki's body as they scoured the living room for evidence—Simone was ready to jump out of her skin. The weapon this time had been a knotted cotton cord—a tieback from one of the heavy living room drapes—wrapped tightly enough around Nikki's neck to strangle her.

"So you want me to believe you were just in the wrong place at the wrong time? Twice?"

"I wasn't alone today. As I said, Cass waited outside, but she can back me up on the fact that the door was open and Nikki was already dead."

"Yeah, well, the word of an ex-con isn't normally considered reliable."

Simone glanced over into the kitchen and saw Detective Jamal Walker questioning Cass. Cass looked nervous—no wonder if she'd served time before. Not that Simone believed Cass had been any more guilty of a crime than she herself was.

"I told you we were at a meeting of the Chicago Philanthropic Club until an hour ago," Simone protested. "Members of which are upstanding citizens and can all vouch for us."

"I know who you really are, Ms. Burke. I know all about your family. Your brother. You can try to lose yourself among the upstanding citizens of the world, but in the end, it won't save you."

The words were a blow to Simone. She'd lived her life in exemplary fashion—she'd never had so much as a speeding ticket. Or a parking ticket, for that matter! This was another reminder that she couldn't divorce herself from the DeNali name and all that it entailed.

"I didn't do anything wrong!" she insisted. "I certainly didn't kill anyone!"

"The Albright woman has been dead for longer than

a couple of hours. She's still in her nightgown. You said coming here was your idea. You could have done the job earlier and then brought along a patsy to stand up for you. Too bad you didn't know Cassandra Freed already had a record."

His continuing accusations left Simone speechless and light-headed.

Could they really pin this murder on her?

And if they did, would they add charges for Al Cecchi's murder, as well?

She was fighting a rising fear that threatened to choke her when the door opened again and Detective John Logan walked in, Gideon right behind him.

"Logan, what're you doing here?" Norelli's gaze took in the other detective's companion, and his expression grew grim. "The both of you?"

"You remember Gideon, owner of Club Undercover," Logan said. "I did security for him for a while when I was on leave. He has an interest—"

"He's a civilian!"

"He's with me."

"And this is my case."

Logan gave Norelli an agreeable smile. "No one said it wasn't."

"You called in a civilian?"

Gideon clarified the situation. "Cass called me and I called Logan."

"So you're here for the dame."

Gideon's gaze locked with Simone's when he said, "I'm here to make sure *the ladies* are all right."

"Yeah, yeah, stay then. Don't move and don't touch anything. Most of all, don't be a pain in my—"

"Detective?" One of the crime scene investigators waved Norelli over.

"We're not done," he said to Simone before leaving her, Logan following close on his heels.

Simone felt as if she could breathe again, at least until Gideon whispered, "What the hell were you thinking?"

"I didn't know Nikki was dead."

"Cass said she had a bad feeling, but you came inside anyway."

"What's the difference? If I hadn't come in, we still would have had to make the call to the police, and I still would have been under suspicion."

"But there wouldn't be any trace of you at the scene."

He thought they would nail her for this murder. No doubt Logan had told him so on the way over here; being a cop, Logan would surely know.

Simone's stomach knotted more tightly.

She glanced over at Cass, who was sitting alone, withdrawn and appearing all too vulnerable. Simone thought to go into the other room to talk to Cass, but before she could, Norelli was back and in her face.

"We got a time of death somewhere between midnight and three in the morning," he said. "So where were *you* last night, Ms. Burke?"

Simone's eyes widened. For a good part of that time, she'd been in Al Cecchi's office. Not that she could tell him that. Horrified, she realized that she was damned if she told him the truth and damned if she didn't.

"She was with me," Gideon said, making it sound very, very personal. "Consider me her alibi."

ALIBI OR NOT, Simone knew that Norelli still had his sights on her as his prime suspect.

Once again, she was told not to leave town.

What would Gideon expect in return for telling a half-truth? she wondered. Had he gotten pleasure in making her squirm with his intimation about them? Surely he wouldn't expect *that* from her.

As Simone headed for the door, she avoided him, which swung her closer to the living room. She didn't want to see what was going on there, but it was like passing a car wreck—she simply had to look one more time.

The investigative team was still busily working. One man was checking out furniture, and Simone realized he was looking for fingerprints. Suddenly it hit her that he was examining Cecchi's desk, the top of which was half torn off and hanging from a hinge. It was a shame that the beautiful antique had been so badly mangled.

An even bigger shame that Nikki Albright was dead.

Knees suddenly weak, Simone couldn't get out of the house fast enough.

She got down the steps and moved to the curb looking for a taxi. In a mental fog, she didn't object when Gideon said, "I'll take you home."

"I'll give Cass a ride," Logan volunteered.

"That would be great." Cass turned to Simone. "Are you all right?"

"Not really. And I'm sorry I dragged you into—"

"No need for an apology. I'm glad I was there to speak up for you."

If the police even believe the word of someone who has been in prison before, Simone thought. Smiling through her doubts, trying to tame her fears, she gave the other woman a quick hug, then asked, "You didn't have any unusual feelings in there, right?"

"You mean did I see the murderer?" Cass shook her head. "I tried to get an image, but as usual…"

Simone knew there was more. "You sensed something?"

"It's all confused."

"Try me."

Cass shook her head. "It's as if the murderer's identity were hidden."

"Hidden?"

"Like I said, it's confusing."

Logan said, "There's no confusion about one thing. It really is too much of a coincidence that both Cecchi and the Albright woman were murdered within days of each other. If it had just been Nikki Albright, Norelli probably would have come to the conclusion that she'd interrupted a burglary. But with the two victims both having been at the fund-raiser…it seems the murders may be connected, and with Simone finding both bodies, Norelli is sure to put some heat on her."

"What can we do to take it off?" Gideon asked.

"Find the murderer. Is there an Albright-Cecchi connection?" Logan asked her.

"Absolutely," Simone said. "Al got Nikki's ex, Sam Albright, off on charges of molesting a minor—a teenage boy—and Nikki was angry because she thought it reduced her divorce settlement. That's why she was so set on getting Al's desk at the auction."

"Then that's where I'll start."

"One more thing," Simone added. "At the party, Sam overheard Nikki telling me about their divorce settlement. He told her to watch her mouth and she asked him what he was going to do to stop her from talking."

"Death would do it," Logan said. "I'll see what I can dig up on him in CPD records, whether or not he's been brought in for anything else. Maybe I'll pay him a friendly visit."

Simone suspected Logan's version of friendly was darker than Norelli's. Well, good. Having a cop on her side was at least one thing in her favor.

"What else?" Gideon asked him.

"For now, it's all I've got. Too bad there were no witnesses." Logan shook his head, opened the passenger door for Cass and got behind the wheel.

As he took off, a childish cry caught Simone's attention and she was suddenly focusing on the kids who were still playing outside.

"Wait a minute…" She walked over to them. "Hey, there."

"What's going on?" the oldest boy asked, looking past her to the official vehicles lined up at the curb.

"Someone broke in next door late last night. Did any of you hear anything?"

"Like a noise?" another kid asked.

"Right. Maybe around midnight or later."

"We don't stay up that late, lady."

"Mom would kill us."

"I heard something," the littlest girl said, her face spreading into a wide grin. "An' I saw him."

The pulse in Simone's throat pounded as she asked, "Saw who?" The murderer?

"Santa Claus!"

The other kids laughed and one of them said, "She's always seeing Santa."

Of course the little girl would, with Christmas two weeks away. Throat tightening, Simone said, "Thanks."

Gideon didn't comment until they were in the car and on their way. Then he asked, "What made you think the kids might know something?"

"Kids are more observant than a lot of people realize." *Especially someone who doesn't even know he has a kid,* she thought, trying not to feel guilty about not wanting to tell him about Drew.

"And imaginative."

Realizing he'd heard the little girl say she saw Santa, Simone said, "You'd be surprised at how observant they can be, though. Drew always seemed to know what was going on with our neighbors—he was certainly more in tune with the local goings-on than I ever was."

"Drew...your son."

"Right."

Simone mentally flogged herself for bringing up

their son. What if Gideon started questioning her about him? She was so distracted by the possibility that it took her a while to realize he'd turned up Milwaukee Avenue.

"Taking the long route to my place?"

"We're not going to your place."

"But you said you'd take me home."

"I did. And I am. To mine. We need to keep on this investigation, Simone. Your finding Nikki Albright made it even more critical."

Knowing he was correct didn't make her any more comfortable with the thought of being alone with him. But if she protested, he would sense her discomfort. She didn't want Gideon to have the upper hand, so she just swallowed her objection.

He said, "Before leaving the club, I gave Gabe the list of names we pulled from Cecchi's files, so he's already working on the security checks."

"What about the committee members and the party guests?" Lists that he would have obtained before the event.

Simone felt odd checking out the women she'd known for years, but everyone had secrets.

"Those, too, but they'll take longer," Gideon said. "One of the things he's doing is cross-checking them. I want to know if any of Cecchi's clients showed up at the party."

Simone was impressed by his thoroughness. Gideon had thought of everything, it seemed. "So what's next?"

"There isn't a *next* until we get some answers. We need some information to follow up."

"I thought the point of your abducting me was to work on the case."

"Abducting?" He sounded amused. "A bit of an exaggeration, wouldn't you say? And after this morning, you could use a little downtime before we start again. Definitely some food."

"I'm not hungry."

"Then you can watch me eat," he said, parking the car in front of an old Wicker Park conversion. "This is it. Home, sweet home."

As she followed him into the former warehouse and up to the top floor loft, Simone felt her wariness grow. This getting-personal business—knowing that Gideon had a comfortable if too-modern-for-her-taste loft apartment—was dangerous. She couldn't chance getting too comfortable around him.

She wanted Gideon's help finding the murderer—or murderers. They still didn't know if the two deaths were connected. What she didn't want was him getting too close, or his figuring out what she didn't want him to know.

Trapped. Feeling trapped frightened her. Simone knew there were many ways to be trapped. If Gideon learned they'd had a son as a result of their one night together, what then?

She would never be free of him.

Was she trading a jail cell for a different kind of prison?

THE KITCHEN WAS Gideon's favorite area of the loft. Cooking had always relaxed him, and so he'd made certain to get a place with a state-of-the-art kitchen—granite countertops, island stove and workspace, patterned ceramic floor, stainless steel appliances. He added chopped garlic and mushrooms and fresh tomatoes to the pan in which olive oil was already sizzling.

"Can you really resist this smell?" he asked Simone, who sat on a stool on the other side of the counter. She hadn't relaxed yet.

"In my wildest dreams, I wouldn't have taken you for a man who cooks."

"Hopefully your dreams are wilder than that." Her nostrils flared at the implication and he was aroused. "What would you take me for?" he asked. "Someone who has everything done for him?" He checked another pot filled with bubbling water and hand-cut pasta he'd brought from the club; the pasta was almost tender enough. "When I struck out on my own, one of my first jobs was as a short-order cook."

"So how did you get from there to here?"

"A combination of hard work and luck. I went to college, but I was always starting over. I never could get a degree because I had to keep changing identities. I couldn't exactly claim credits earned under another name."

"How frustrating for you," she said, sounding sincere. "At least you were free to keep moving."

"You think so? Free?" He poured the pasta into a colander. "I couldn't use my own name. I couldn't stay in one place. I couldn't make a real life."

"You seem to have one now."

His gaze intent on her, he said, "It's a new start. And this time, I assure you I'm not going anyplace."

Simone looked away, but not before he noted something disturbing reflected in her eyes. Fear? Of him? Maybe she *should* fear him. Maybe *he* should want revenge. But with Simone close enough to touch, revenge was the last thing on his mind.

He tossed the pasta with the mushrooms and tomatoes, then divided the food onto two plates and set them on the counter between them.

"A little Parmesan?" he asked. "And don't say you're not hungry."

She sniffed. "Actually, I believe I'm starving."

Passing the bowl of grated cheese, he then got the garlic bread from the toaster oven and filled a basket. When he held it out to her, she made a little sound at the back of her throat. A moan. Sounded like sex. He was ready to have some.

He watched her eat. Simone was not one of those women who picked at her food; she ate with gusto.

Just as he remembered.

He remembered so many things about her. About them. They'd defied their families to be with each other. A modern Romeo and Juliet fairy tale—that's what friends had said about them. Too bad it had turned into a horror story just like the Shakespearean tragedy.

"How bad was it?" Simone suddenly asked. "The moving around and starting over."

"Mind-numbing at times. But it wasn't all bad. I got to live in New Mexico for a while. That was different."

"Santa Fe?"

Gideon laughed. "Hardly. I didn't have the bucks back then. Try Taos—slower-paced, more Old West, filled with odd characters. I lived practically for nothing on a commune with a bunch of old hippies for a while. I tended their llamas until I got a job as a bartender and could afford my own room in a boarding house."

"Is that where you learned how to run a club?"

He shook his head. "That happened years later, when I landed in Vegas. I was an assistant manager in a casino nightclub, then got promoted to manager. I was good at it."

"Managing and owning are two different things. So what made you decide to start a club of your own?"

"The roll of some very lucky dice. I rarely gambled—I mean, working in the business, you know the odds are against you. It was an aberration—the playing, as well as the winning—and I knew it wouldn't happen again, so I took the money and ran. Opportunity brought me right here, so here I am." Opportunity and the desire to take back his real life. He sat back and studied her as he said, "You seem to have made a real life for yourself."

"I may lose my home."

"I don't mean things. I mean people. Friends. Family."

"I have my son."

"And your brother." As much as Michael hated him, he loved his sister. Gideon had no doubts about that.

"But not my father."

"He's still alive."

"Incarcerated for a crime he didn't commit."

Gideon stiffened. "I didn't lie on the stand, Simone. I saw him shoot and kill my father."

"It was night. The weather was bad. You had to have made a mistake."

"Why? Because *Papa* says so?"

She threw down her fork. "Papa never lied to me."

"You don't know that."

"He may have done things that were against the law, but I know he didn't kill your father."

"You're blind, Simone. When it comes to your family, you just don't want to see the truth."

"Can't you concede the possibility of an error?"

"No."

"Well, neither can I." She slid off her stool. "I need to get home. My son will be expecting me. Don't bother getting up. This time, I *will* grab a taxi."

He watched her put on her coat with giant tugs. The garment twisted around and frustrated her, but she didn't give up.

"How could you do it, Simone? After what we shared, how we felt about each other, how could you turn around and make a life with another man so soon? How could you sleep with him, have his kid when I know you loved me?"

This time, he was sure he saw panic in her eyes as she finished pulling on her coat. She grabbed her shoulder bag and started for the door. He put out a hand to stop her so they could finish this, but she ripped her arm away.

"Don't touch me!"

Gideon simply stared at her. For a moment, she went still, as if she were a deer caught in headlights. Then, her expression crumpling, a sob escaping her, she rushed out of the place, slamming the door behind her.

If he didn't know better, he would swear she still felt for him what he felt for her. He would swear she'd never wanted to marry another man.

Then why had she?

Somehow, he'd missed connecting some of the dots.

Chapter Nine

As she flagged down a taxi on Damen Avenue, Simone fought back tears. She'd come so close to breaking down in front of Gideon that it scared her. Hopefully, he thought she was upset over their argument about Papa—which she was.

But she was even more upset by his angry questions.

The truth was that she'd still been in love with Gideon when she'd married David. David had accepted that. He'd said she would learn to love him, and she had, if not in the way he'd wanted.

How could she when Drew had been a daily reminder of the man who'd awakened her heart before he'd crushed it?

Not that she could tell Gideon any of that. Let him believe what he wanted. She had to put her son first. She couldn't destroy his world, his memories of the only father he'd ever known, the father he'd adored.

She understood that kind of love because it was the

way she still felt about her own father. She knew Papa had never been a law-abiding citizen, that he'd even been involved with violence, but she had to believe that he drew the line somewhere—at cold-blooded murder.

Drew…she had to concentrate on her son.

He was a growing teenager who was always hungry. So putting her mind to his needs, Simone had the taxi leave her off at the local market, then walked the two blocks home with several bags of groceries.

Knowing Drew would find out about the second murder and her involvement soon enough, Simone vowed to tell him herself. Not a pleasant task. The very thought of giving him more bad news—this kind of bad news—made her stomach knot. Somehow she would find a way to do it.

What she couldn't do was make him understand, not when she didn't understand how she'd found herself in the middle of such a nightmare.

Simone was approaching the house when she realized she couldn't find her house keys. What the heck had she done with them? Normally she kept them in her right-hand pocket, but they weren't there; she had too many bags to juggle to easily find them.

She was annoyed, but thankful she kept a spare key to the kitchen door wedged in an opening under the potting bench on the back porch. Not that she'd ever had to use it before. But Drew had, several times.

She was halfway down the narrow gangway when a furtive movement somewhere in back raised the hair at the back of her neck. Though she slowed her footsteps and narrowed her gaze, she couldn't see anything.

"Drew?" she called out, her pulse skittering. "What are you doing back there?"

No answer.

Maybe she'd imagined the movement. Or maybe it had been the neighbor's cat streaking through her yard. Just in case...she stopped to listen for any unusual sounds.

Nothing.

Puffing a breath through cold lips, she cautiously continued into the backyard, her gaze roaming and digging into every corner.

Empty.

Her imagination was really getting to her. Making her jumpy. And no wonder, considering what she'd been through in the past few days.

Once on the porch, Simone set the bags down on the potting bench. Even as she bent over to feel for the key, she sensed someone was there, cloaked in darkness...waiting...watching. Fingers fumbling, skin crawling, she stopped what she was doing and straightened.

"Who's there?" she called, even as a dark silhouette slid out from a tree near the alley. Before the man could get away, she caught a glimpse of pale hair and, certain it was Michael's bodyguard, called out, "Ulf Nachtmann, what are you doing in my backyard?"

Ulf stopped and turned to face her. Stepping closer, he threw up his hands in a sheepish gesture. "I was simply checking on you for your brother. Mr. DeNali is concerned about your safety."

The bodyguard was wreathed in shadow, his bulk making a scary figure despite his innocent act.

"Michael told you to scare me half to death?"

"You weren't here, so I waited for you to come home to make sure you were okay. I was trying to be discreet. How could I have known you would come to the back door?"

"Tell my brother I don't need…never mind, I'll do it myself."

Adrenaline still pumping, Simone turned her back on the guard, fetched the hidden key and unlocked the kitchen door. When she glanced into the yard, Ulf was gone. Or so it seemed. For all she knew, he could be behind the garage or waiting in the gangway. Was tonight the first night he'd been watching her? If not, had he seen her with Gideon?

Oh, great!

Replacing the key, she grabbed her bags, set them down in the kitchen, grabbed a phone and speed-dialed her brother.

Michael picked up on the first ring. "DeNali."

Without so much as a greeting, Simone said, "Tell your watchdog to back off, Michael. Now."

"Well, good evening to you, too."

"Don't avoid the subject."

"You'll have to be more specific."

"Ulf nearly scared me to death. I don't want a bodyguard, Michael, so please, don't send him around again!"

"I didn't. If Ulf has been playing maverick—"

"Then fire him!"

With that, Simone hung up on her brother so he would know she was serious. Taking a couple of deep breaths to release her anger, she emptied the bags and put the groceries away.

Luckily she had time to change, shower and cook up a couple of burgers before Drew walked in the door. She wasn't hungry, but she would try to eat with her son because that was the normal thing to do.

"Hey, Mom," he said, the sullenness of the previous day gone when he swooped to kiss her cheek.

"Have a good day?" she asked before she saw the bruise on his cheek. "Honey, what happened to you?"

"Ah, nothing. I just ran into something."

"Like a fist?"

"It's nothing."

Nothing…she bit back the demand that he tell her what had happened and hoped that he would volunteer the information.

"You need to ice it."

"I already did. I'm not a kid anymore, you know."

He was still sixteen, but she didn't remind him of that. He was growing up fast. He used to tell her about everything, including the fights. Either he was feeling too grown up…or the fight had been about her.

"So what about your day?" he asked. "Are you okay?"

At least he'd gotten over his pique of the night before, and his concern had kicked in.

"My day started great," she told him. "The fund-raiser made even more money than expected…"

His expression concerned, Drew asked, "What about the rest of the day?"

"Honey, I don't know how to tell you this except straight out. I found Nikki Albright dead."

"Dead? Not murdered?"

Simone nodded.

"And you found her…like Mr. Cecchi? They don't suspect you did it, do they?"

"I—I'm afraid so. We're DeNalis, Drew. We might not use the name, but you know the police don't differenti-ate."

Thankfully, she'd talked to her son about what it meant to be a DeNali last year when he'd had a run-in with an officer after he'd been in a fight at school. The officer had found out his connection to Michael and had made assumptions that weren't true.

Drew knew that his grandfather had run some ille-gal businesses and that he'd been imprisoned for Frank Ruscetti's murder. She'd told him this so he would un-derstand that if he ever got into trouble, people might assume the trouble was his fault, whether or not it was.

"Does Uncle Mike know?"

"I'm not sure."

She wouldn't put it past her brother to have a few cops in his back pocket who would supply him with information.

"He'll help you, Mom, you know he will. All you have to do is say the word."

Simone's voice was tight when she said, "It's not your uncle's job to get me out of trouble. Well, maybe he could find me a criminal lawyer if I needed one."

"What good is having power if you can't use it?"

His question took away her breath. Drew's expression was angry and confused. He wanted to protect her, and apparently he didn't care how.

"Drew, you scare me when you talk like that. Your father and I taught you better. We taught you to stand for doing the right thing."

"If the cops arrest you, that won't be right, will it?"

"No, it won't, because I didn't kill anyone."

"Neither did Grandpa—that's what you said—and look where he is."

"I'm not going to end up behind bars," Simone assured him, although she knew that she might. "And I don't want you to worry about something that's not going to happen."

Drew accepted her bravado, but she could almost hear his mind working.

If he were desperate enough to go to Michael for help, then all the sacrifices she'd made to give him a good, safe life would have been for naught.

GIDEON WAS in a dark mood when he returned to the club a couple of hours later. He was still wondering why he'd pressed the services of Team Undercover on Simone. Though she didn't deserve to be convicted for something she hadn't done, she certainly didn't seem to appreciate his help in clearing her name. Then again, what had he expected from her—that she would be so grateful that she would simply decide he'd been telling the truth about her father all along?

Trying to keep as detached as he'd been while working on the team's previous cases was proving to be impossible. He would simply have to try harder.

With that resolution made, he entered the security office where Gabe sat before the computer, exactly as he'd been hours earlier when the call had come in from Cass.

"How's it going?"

Gabe spun around in his chair. "I got a few interesting hits. More interesting follow-up."

"As in…"

"The napkin you gave me…the phone number belongs to a woman named Josie Ralston. She lives in a highrise over on Hampden Court. I happen to know the security guy there."

"And?"

"He says Ms. Ralston only moved in a couple of months ago. And she's not responsible for the rent."

"Cecchi?"

Gabe nodded.

"The mistress he denied having."

"Bingo."

"Good work. I'll need that address. What else?"

"This is even more interesting. Anthony Viglio, supposedly a new case, gave Cecchi a huge retainer, so he immediately caught my interest."

"And?"

"The man's dead."

Gideon started. "Another murder?"

"Car accident. He was buried six months ago. A dead man hired Al Cecchi to represent him."

Gabe handed Gideon a printout of the obituary with a photo of a small dark-haired, dark-eyed man.

"A dead man hiring a lawyer—that's fresh. How big a retainer?"

"Half a mil."

Gideon whistled. "Our dead man must have done something really bad, huh? Got right up from the grave and…what crime had he supposedly not committed that he needed Cecchi's services?"

"What else? Murder."

Though they couldn't figure out how this worked into the case, Gideon had a gut feeling it somehow did. Maybe once he brought Simone up to speed on this supposed client, she would remember why the name had seemed familiar to her.

Gideon was about to call Simone to ask, but decided instead to show up on her doorstep. First he would give her some time to cool down. He had some phone calls to make and checks to write to vendors, so for the next few hours he busied himself with club business.

The whole time he tried to work, he was distracted with thoughts of Simone.

He wished he were over her. He had hoped that being in contact with her would finally get her out of his system. No such luck. She had turned out to be as fierce a mother as she had been a daughter. She was all about family, something he missed and wanted. He made an occasional call to his mother or sister, but he hadn't seen either of them in a few years. He didn't think he'd ever fill the void in his life...until Simone had come back into it.

Wondering how Simone felt about him in her heart of hearts drove him to distraction. He would swear she still cared, but what did that mean exactly? She'd turned her back on him once. When this was over, would she be able to cut him out of her life as easily as she had the last time? Maybe he was crazy but he wanted her more than ever, no matter that she was still misguided in believing her father instead of him.

DeNali loyalty—there was nothing stronger. He'd conquered it once when he'd won her heart...and then had lost to it when he'd testified against Richard DeNali.

Unable to concentrate on work any longer, Gideon left the club and drove toward Lincoln Park West. Finding an empty metered space on Clark Street was like winning the lottery. Walking, he passed nearby store windows glowing with Christmas displays and lampposts dripping with garlands of pine.

Turning the corner onto Simone's street, Gideon admired the century-old homes and two flats. They, too, were dressed in holiday decorations. Halfway down the block, he arrived at Simone's and bounded up her front steps. He noticed the tree in the window had lights but no ornaments. Seeing her through the living room window, he knocked at the door rather than ringing the bell.

Simone started and when she peered out the window, she frowned at him.

The frown was still in place when she opened the

front door halfway and wedged herself in the opening. "Gideon! What are you doing here?"

"I have some interesting information."

Simone just stood there, almost as if she were debating letting him inside. Apparently she hadn't yet cooled off from their earlier disagreement. She appeared perturbed rather than angry, but soon any expression was replaced by a neutral mask that was becoming all too familiar to him.

She backed away from the door. "Come in."

Gideon stepped inside. The room had an inviting warmth with its fire and twinkling Christmas tree lights that immediately made him feel at home. Too bad he couldn't say the same for Simone herself. From her, he felt a definite chill.

"So what is it?" she asked.

"Aren't you going to take my coat?" He removed it and handed it to her.

"If you must." She hung it on a wooden tree to one side of the door.

"Offer me a seat?"

Her mouth tightened. "Take your pick."

"A glass of brandy?"

"Gideon!"

She was glaring at him, her green eyes glittering. And he was suddenly turned on. He wanted to take her right here, in front of the fireplace.

As if she were a mind-reader, she gasped and stepped back. "If you have something important to tell me, out with it!"

He leaned against the back of the couch that faced the fireplace. "Anthony Viglio is dead."

"What?" The delicate skin between her eyebrows furrowed. "Viglio…one of Al's clients. How? When?"

He handed her the printout with the photo. "Car accident months before he hired Cecchi."

She stared down at the paper in hand. "I—I don't understand."

"I don't, either. Apparently a dead man hired the firm to represent him. You thought you recognized the name. Anything more on that?"

She shook her head. "I know the name, but not why. I'm sorry."

"Think on it some more."

"That's it, then?"

"In a rush to see me go?"

"No, of course not. I'm just tired. Was there something else?"

There was. With her. Definitely. He could sense it. Only what?

"The number on that napkin I found in Cecchi's desk—it belonged to a woman named Josie Ralston. She lives two blocks from here on Hampden Court," he said, momentarily distracted by footsteps overhead. Then he realized they must belong to her son Drew. "Guess who held the lease on her apartment?"

"You're saying that it was Al? That Teresa wasn't delusional?"

"Apparently not. I thought we could walk over there and pay Ms. Ralston a visit."

Before Simone could answer, footsteps quickly thundered down a nearby staircase. Simone started and whipped around. Gideon followed her lead and zeroed in on the teenager who was rushing to the front door.

"I'm late, Mom. Gotta go. Charlie's waiting for me."

"Be home before eleven."

Drew paused and stared at Gideon for a moment; his frown was much like his mother's, but his narrowing eyes weren't. Simone's were green; the boy's were blue, nearly electric. He pushed a lock of blue-black hair from a neatly chiseled face.

Then Drew was gone.

And, mind racing, Gideon was left staring after him.

"Where were we?" Simone asked, sounding a bit breathless.

Panicky?

When he faced her, she tried to go all neutral on him again, but she couldn't.

Gideon felt as if he'd been punched in the gut. Looking at Drew was like looking in the mirror a couple of decades ago.

Why hadn't she told him?

Simone had gone stiff and seemed to have trouble breathing. Why shouldn't she after what she'd done? It all became clear to him now—why she'd married another man so fast. Now he knew what...*Drew*.

"Why didn't you ever tell me you were pregnant with my child?" he nearly shouted.

Simone shrugged and moved away from him, saying, "Drew is David's son."

He caught her shoulder and spun her around. "That's a lie."

"David and Drew couldn't have been closer!"

"Only because you let him believe the kid was his."

She licked her lips and he could see her swallow hard. It seemed she wanted to lie to him again, but couldn't make herself do it.

Finally, she said, "David knew."

"Well that's great. Did everyone know but me?"

"I was going to tell you…I tried to tell you that last night…"

"Then why didn't you?"

"I was scared. I'd just found out for sure myself and didn't know what to say. And then later…how could I tell you after what happened?"

"I don't know. How about, 'Joey, I'm sorry about your father. I know this is a bad time to tell you this, but I'm pregnant.'"

"You betrayed me!"

"Oh, that's right. You thought I was lying about your father killing mine. So you lied to me, kept my son from me. Payback, Simone?" he asked, stepping closer. The heat of her anger nearly seared him, but he was furious with her, too. "Is that what this was? I took your father from you, so you took my son in return?"

It all made sense now, those emotions he'd sworn she had for him—the push-pull that made her want him and yet reject him. She might have been able to punish him, but she hadn't been able to forget what they'd had. Seventeen years ago, even though she'd loved him, she'd refused to see him lest he figure out she was carrying his kid. Maybe she loved him still. He simply didn't understand how she'd been able to do it.

Or had it been...

"Michael," he murmured, the realization hitting him. "Was it his idea for you to stay away from me?"

"Michael was only trying to protect me," Simone said stiffly. She wrapped her arms around her middle as if she were trying to protect herself. "He kept me safe. Away from the reporters—"

"And away from me." A no-brainer. "Did you ever think of telling me?"

"What good would it have done? You had disappeared. Even if I had decided to tell you, how would I have found you?"

He kept his voice even when he said, "So in the end, Michael won. He got you away from me the way he wanted all along."

"It wasn't like that!"

She'd always been blind to her father's and brother's faults. And to their manipulation.

"Is that why Michael funded Cecchi and Burke? Al Cecchi wanted to start off on his own, and your brother saw an opportunity to keep you away from me forever. Did he use the law firm to buy you your husband?"

Her hand came out of nowhere. One second it was at her side, the next it connected with his face. Anger made her stronger than he had imagined. The slap jerked his head to the side and made him take a step away from her.

They glared at each other; their eyes communicated to one another.

But Gideon wanted more.

He wanted answers.

Waiting until he trusted himself to speak calmly, he asked, "Well?"

For a moment, he thought she might spit in his face and tell him to leave. He watched a surge of emotions play over her face. And then her eyes turned shiny with tears.

"David was always interested in me," she said. "But I never went out with him because I had you. After Papa was arrested, he was there. And yes, Michael encouraged me to see him. And when David proposed, Michael encouraged me to marry him, because he knew I wanted to keep my baby and I was too young to be a single parent. I didn't want my child raised as a DeNali. So I agreed to marry David if he would leave the family business, which he gladly did for me."

David must have really loved Simone to start over.

"So Drew believes David was his father?"

"David *was* his father in every way that counted."

"What about me? Don't I count for anything?"

Simone was shaking her head at him, looking more scared than he'd ever seen her. No matter that he tried to harden himself against her, Gideon felt his chest tighten and gut knot in response.

"You can't tell him," Simone said softly. It was more of a plea than a demand. "Drew adored David. He was devastated when David died. You would take away the only father he's ever known. You would destroy him."

"You don't know that."

"You don't know that you wouldn't."

"Drew needs a father." As *he'd* needed the father who'd been denied him.

"If you tell him…are you willing to chance destroying a young man's life?"

"You mean the way mine was?"

"That's on you."

So they were back to square one.

"I only told the truth, Simone. Loving you and telling the truth were my only crimes."

Her eyes were teary and she pressed her lips together, no doubt to keep herself from crying. Gideon couldn't believe she wanted to cut him out of his son's life now that he knew. David was dead; nothing would bring the man back.

But what if she was correct?

The thought of destroying another young life… Drew was even younger than he had been…Gideon couldn't shoulder that responsibility.

He nodded curtly. "If he finds out, it won't be from me."

He was used to being alone, after all. Any illusion that he might have had about him and Simone had come apart in shreds.

Instead, he had another reason to mourn.

Chapter Ten

As they walked in silence to Josie Ralston's Hampden Court highrise, Simone got herself back under control.

It wasn't like her to lose it. She'd hidden from the past for so long she'd fooled herself into believing it held no power over her anymore. Knowing that Gideon could so easily take her back to a place that meant only pain made her doubt her decision to let him help her.

And what he could do to Drew...

Simone's pulse sped up when he put a hand in the middle of her back as they turned the corner onto Hampden. Then his hand dropped away, leaving her with a hollow feeling.

Would it always be this way? she wondered, spotting the highrise. Many of the units had been bought as investment properties—they gave a far better return than a bank and were safer than the stock market—and had been rented out, including the apartment Al had found for his mistress.

As they approached the building, Simone finally

broke the silence. "So, do you think she'll just let us up?"

"I wouldn't count on it, but not to worry—I made other arrangements."

"Such as?"

"The security guard is an off-duty cop, a friend of Gabe's. He'll let us into the foyer. We can just show up at the Ralston woman's door and knock."

Which could get the security guard into trouble if Josie complained to the management, Simone worried, before reminding herself of the trouble she would be in if they didn't get some answers.

"She still won't have to let us in."

"Hey, I did my part. The rest is up to you. We're both strangers, but no doubt she'll respond better to a woman than a man," Gideon said. "Besides, I'm sure you can be persuasive if you try."

His words mocked her. Was he thinking about the way she'd convinced him not to tell Drew who he was? For a moment, guilt ate at Simone. No matter that she'd originally meant to tell him about her pregnancy, in the end, she'd hidden it from him—hidden his son from him.

Maybe she had given in too readily to Michael's influence in the matter. But if she'd been truthful, what then? She never would have agreed to marry the man who'd put her father in prison for something he didn't do. She couldn't fathom that he would have wanted to marry *her*. Caught between feuding families, their child would have been the one to suffer.

She'd done the only thing she could have, Simone assured herself, as the doorman let them in and they stopped before the security desk. As Gideon spoke to the guard, she thought about how she could get the Ralston woman to open her door to them. She needed a convincing argument.

Even before they entered the elevator, she had an idea. Gideon pressed the button to the top floor, and as they stepped out, Simone noted there were only two doors—one on either side of the hallway—and realized Al had provided his mistress with a penthouse apartment.

Forcing a smile to her stiff lips, she noted the door had a doorbell and intercom. She stepped in front of the peephole as she rang.

A moment later, a husky voice via the intercom asked, "Who is it?"

"I represent Cecchi and Burke Law Offices, Ms. Ralston, and I need to speak to you about your lease."

The door opened immediately. "If you're here to tell me I gotta leave—" Josie's eyes widened when she realized two people stood outside her door. "Hey, what is this?"

Surprised by the familiar purple-streaked dark hair and equally familiar stomach exposed by low-rider jeans and a jewel-studded crop top, Simone went wide-eyed, as well. She'd seen this woman at Club Undercover…with her brother. This woman was Michael's alibi.

"I think you'd better let us in, Ms. Ralston," Gideon said.

Simone blinked and tore her gaze away from the stunning navel ring that she would swear was a real ruby. One Al bought for her? Josie clenched her jaw and Simone thought she was going to refuse to talk to them.

But Al's mistress backed away from the door on her spindly ankle-strap sandals and said, "All right, come in, but make it quick. I'm in a hurry. I have a…an appointment to keep."

At this hour? Did she mean a date? Simone wondered. And with Al not even in the grave. Then it occurred to her that Michael could be that "appointment."

Simone didn't like this link between her brother and Al's mistress.

Nor did she like the fact that Al Cecchi had spent so much money—David's share of the business—on this woman.

The penthouse apartment had the touch of a professional designer. Not that purple furniture and hot pink trimmings were her cup of tea. But she recognized the complex floor-to-ceiling window treatments from *Metropolitan Home* magazine. Added to designer furniture were several sculptures—also not to her taste—that had probably cost a fortune.

All this could have paid for Drew's tuition until he graduated from high school.

So Simone couldn't help but be resentful as the other woman stood there, arms crossed over her exposed stomach, saying, "You know, this is really inconvenient, your just showing up here like this."

"Should I have waited to speak to you at the wake?" Simone asked.

"Wake?"

"Al's. Tomorrow night. You *are* planning on being there, aren't you."

Josie made a face and shrugged her shoulders. "Uh, right. The old bat he was married to would really appreciate my showing up for her party."

Simone wanted to smack her, but smiled instead.

"So then, here we are," Gideon said.

Josie frowned at him. "You look familiar."

"Club Undercover—I own it."

A flicker of something Simone couldn't interpret slid through the woman's eyes before she shuttered her response and brushed by him. She settled in an armchair and indicated the purple couch. "So, sit."

Making herself as comfortable as she could considering the circumstances, Simone introduced herself and added, "My late husband was Al's partner. So now I'm one of the owners of the firm and therefore have control over the lease to this place and everything in it."

Simone wasn't certain that was correct—if Al had given his mistress the furniture, it might very well be hers legally, even if he had stolen the money from David's share of the business to pay for his largesse—but she wanted to put the other woman on rocky footing.

"So you're what? Here to evict me? I know my rights. You have to give me proper notice. Albert told me so."

"Albert?"

She waved her hand. "He insisted his women always called him by his full name."

His women...how many had there been? Simone wondered.

"We're here for information," Gideon said smoothly. "You cooperate with us and there won't be a problem."

"Cooperate how?"

"We're looking for a murderer."

"Hey, look, I had nothing to do with what happened to Albert."

"But you were at the club that night. Why?"

As Gideon grilled Josie, Simone could see the wheels in the other woman's mind spinning. She wasn't answering and no doubt trying to find a way out of telling them anything.

"You want to help find Al's murderer," Simone prompted. "Don't you?"

"Yeah, yeah, of course. But what makes you think I know anything?"

"You were his mistress. Men tend to talk in bed."

"If you think that's all we were doing..." Josie rolled her eyes.

Gideon took over. "But you *did* talk, right?"

"Yeah, sometimes."

"About?"

"Stuff. I don't know."

"Problems with a client? With a friend?"

"You mean like a suspect?"

"Exactly, like a suspect."

Josie was playing dumb, and Simone wondered why. A dumb woman didn't live like this. What did Josie know that she wasn't saying? Perhaps a different tactic was called for.

"Al sure kept you well," she said.

"Yeah, until he ran out of bucks."

Gideon jumped on that. "So his death freed you to look for someone with ready cash."

"Hey, wait a minute! Don't be trying to pin nothing on me!"

"So he ran out of money…when?" Simone asked.

"He got tighter and tighter the last month or so. Said his ship was gonna come in, only it never did," Josie said, her tone resentful.

"What kind of ship?" Simone asked.

"How would I know?"

"We already established that you talked…among other things."

"Al had some kind of deal he was trying to make, but what does it matter what kind if he was just gonna gamble the profits away?"

"He was a serious gambler, then," Gideon said.

"He said it wasn't a problem, that he was just trying to make up for some money he needed to pay back, but he didn't say who he owed. If you ask me, gambling was Albert's drug of choice and had been for a long time. He was just good at hiding it at first."

Simone locked gazes with Gideon and knew he was thinking the same thing she was. Gambling losses…the reason for all those withdrawals…the reason she was broke.

They tried again to get something from Josie on anyone who had a grudge against Al, but her answer held nothing new, only a ring of familiarity. "Hey, he was a lawyer. Coulda been anyone."

Gideon handed her his card. "If you think of anything more specific—threats, warnings, weird phone calls—let me know immediately."

Josie took a sultry pose. "How about I just call you?"

Gideon's eyebrow flicked up in what Simone interpreted as undue interest.

"I'll be in touch about the apartment," Simone told Josie. "I suggest you don't do a disappearing act with any of the inventory."

Hostile replaced sultry. "Don't worry. I'm not going nowhere."

Simone couldn't get out of the place fast enough. And when they hit the street, she accelerated the quick pace despite the fact that it was snowing again and the footing was slippery. Gideon, of course, kept up with her easily.

"In a hurry to get somewhere?" he asked.

"Trying to outrun the truth, that a stranger has David's assets and there's probably nothing I can do about it."

Or nothing she wanted to do about it. Josie Ralston hadn't stolen money that should be supporting her and her son; Al had done that.

"So what do you think Josie meant about Cecchi's ship coming in?" Gideon asked.

"I don't know. An important client with a big retainer, I suppose."

A twitch at the back of her neck made her turn and look over her shoulder through the thickening snow as a large silhouette blended into a doorway. Just someone coming home, she told herself, shaking away the weird feeling.

"I'm assuming the money she said Cecchi was trying to pay back was what he stole from the company," Gideon said. "But a big retainer wouldn't replenish the coffers—it would simply mean additional revenue for the firm. So he must have meant something else, some 'ship' outside of a new client or anything else the firm could bring in."

"Maybe he played the lottery and was hoping his numbers were going to come in," Simone offered sarcastically.

"Yeah, right. A sure thing."

"More likely a big poker game."

"I don't think that's what he meant, either. His ship…" Gideon murmured. "Could he have meant that literally?…like the *Sicilian Breeze*?"

"What? You think he was going to sell it?"

Between his several addictions—mistress and yacht included—Al had managed to bankrupt them. If he wasn't already dead, she would be tempted to strangle the man.

They started down Clark Street before Simone realized Drew could have returned. She didn't want Gideon coming back to her place. "So where did you park?"

"Just ahead at a meter."

"Then you won't mind if we make it a night. I need to do some grocery shopping," she lied, indicating the spot down the street where the market would be if she could see it through the falling snow.

"I can take a hint. You don't want me there when the kid gets back."

She didn't deny it and was relieved that he let the subject drop. Again, the weird feeling—as if she were being watched. When she looked back this time, it was to see a knot of people dance around each other as they came in and out of a store and ended up in a sidewalk jam.

As they approached Gideon's car and stopped, something else occurred to her. "'His women called him Albert,'" she murmured. "That's what Josie said."

"His wife Teresa referred to him as Albert last night," Gideon said. "No doubt she would be thrilled to know she shares that honor."

"With Galen O'Neill, as well."

"The woman in charge of the auction?"

Simone nodded, remembering Galen had called him Albert several times. "The night of party and this morning at the meeting."

"Maybe she didn't know the name had special meaning for him."

"Possibly, but what if she did? Galen seems to be full of surprises. She comes off as this timid, quiet woman. But there's another side to her. Even Cass recognized it."

"Hmm. Sounds like we should pay her a visit and find out. Tomorrow morning?"

Simone nodded. "Tomorrow morning."

They made plans to meet away from her home. Simone said she needed to run some errands first. She was sure Gideon recognized the ploy—that eyebrow was a dead giveaway—but he didn't object and got into his car to go home.

For some reason, feeling the need to keep up the pretext, Simone crossed the street as if she really were going to the market.

Gideon was just driving off when the uneasy sensation returned. Pulse fluttering, she tried to tell herself it was nothing. Indeed, a glance behind her revealed nothing. Heads down against the driving snow, people appeared determined to do their Christmas shopping.

Still, Simone couldn't shake the vague feeling that someone was watching her, following her.

If she changed direction and headed for home, she would be inviting whoever it was to follow her. Her stomach knotted. Being alone on a deserted side street wasn't her smartest option, so she hurried toward the market where there would be plenty of people, lots of light and safety.

That's when she heard the footsteps slap-slapping against the pavement behind, as if someone were trying to catch up to her.

Instinctively, she began to jog.

The footsteps slapped closer.

Heart pounding, Simone ran for all she was worth,

not stopping until she reached the market's entryway, where her path was blocked by a homeless man wrangling a shopping cart—trying to get it through the very posts meant to keep the carts from being taken from the area.

Flipping around to face whoever was behind her, Simone was almost knocked over by a guy in a snow-dusted Santa suit. Without so much as looking her way, he kept going.

The adrenaline rush bottomed out, and Simone's legs grew wobbly. The homeless man gave up on the cart and left, so she was able to get inside the market. Trembling, she stood in the window staring out for a moment. Was someone else there? The sensation had swept out of her along with the adrenaline, and she didn't know if she actually had been in danger or if the creepiness of stumbling over a couple of bodies was just getting to her.

What now? She still had to get home.

Not wanting to step foot outside the door just yet—just in case—Simone headed for the upscale café and got herself a chai latte. A neighbor caught up to her in line and wanted the scoop on the murders.

Normally she would gloss over what she knew and take her leave. But not this time, not when she saw her opportunity to trade some of the sordid details for a safe escort home.

HIS WINDSHIELD WIPERS couldn't keep up with the fast-falling snow any more than Gideon could shake the image of Drew that filled his mind as he drove behind a salt truck.

He had a kid.

That fact changed everything. He didn't know quite how, but it did. Something swelled inside him. Love? He didn't know Drew, so how could he love him? Because Drew was his, he guessed. Drew might not ever know the truth, but Gideon would know and that would have to be enough.

But would it be?

Gideon turned off and headed west, replaying all the what-ifs in his mind.

What if Simone's father hadn't murdered Pop?

What if he and Simone had had a chance to be together?

To raise their son together?

Would he be a different man? Gideon couldn't say. He was who he was. He'd always thought he'd had no regrets.

But now he knew he had a kid...

The more he was with Simone, the more he wanted to be with her. But how? If Drew took a good look at him, surely he would know they were related, exactly what she didn't want. A conundrum, one that took away the possibility of a future with the woman who still made his heart beat faster.

He should be furious with Simone, maybe hate her for keeping Drew from him and allowing someone else to raise him. But he couldn't hate Simone, couldn't continue to be angry. She'd done what she'd done for their son. She'd had her child's best interests at heart.

As hard as it was to swallow, she had Drew's best interest at heart now.

So he would deal with it. Somehow. Somehow he would convince himself that Drew was better off without him. That Simone was, too.

But first, he had to make sure that she didn't go to jail for a murder she didn't commit.

WHEN SIMONE FINALLY made it home safely—no more weird feelings of being watched or followed—she waved goodbye to her neighbor and bounded up the steps. The living room lights shone brightly and glowed invitingly against the snow-covered grounds. Through her front window, Simone spotted the silhouette of a man with his arm around her son's shoulders. Michael must have stopped by again. She looked around for Ulf, but her brother's bodyguard was nowhere in sight.

Thankful that she hadn't let Gideon see her home, Simone bounded up the front steps and unlocked the door. But when she threw it open, she was in for a shock.

The man with Drew was Sam Albright.

Noting her entry, he smiled at her and patted Drew on the shoulder before withdrawing his arm.

"Drew?"

"Hey, Mom!" Drew popped up off the sofa. "Mr. Albright said he needed to talk to you and I figured you would be back soon."

Simone's heart pounded. Drew knew better than to let anyone but Michael or one of his own friends into the house when she wasn't home. Knowing that Albright had gotten away with having relations with a teenage boy, she was hard-pressed to keep her cool.

"Sam." She acknowledged the man in a politely neutral voice before turning her attention back to her son, who seemed perfectly at ease with the man. Relaxing, she asked, "Is your homework done?"

He shrugged. "Mostly."

"Please go finish. It's getting late."

Rolling his eyes, he muttered, "Fine." Then rushed up the stairs saying, "'Night, Mr. Albright."

"'Night, son," Albright said with a familiar wave.

Unable to get rid of the edgy feeling the dead woman's husband gave her—he'd never been in her home before, so why now?—Simone put on a smile and asked, "What can I do for you, Sam?"

Albright's eyes narrowed on her. "You can stay the hell out of my business!"

Reacting to his rancor, Simone gasped, "Pardon me?" and changed her mind about wanting Gideon kept out of her home. At this moment, she wished he were here.

"I know it was you who sicced the cops on me," he snarled. The vehemence of his remark shook loose a lock of blond hair. He smoothed it back into place as he stood and continued his harangue. "You were the only one close enough to overhear what Nikki and I said to each other at the fund-raiser."

Simone thought quickly. She'd never said anything to Norelli or Walker. She had told Gideon, Logan and

Cass what she'd heard. Logan was a detective. Had he shared that information with the official task force?

"Look, Sam, I have nothing against you—"

"You just want to protect your own pretty butt!" he growled, stepping closer.

Simone backed up and, feeling threatened, wildly thought about what she could use to defend herself. The only thing she could come up with was a pointy ornament lying in a box near the tree.

"This is uncalled for."

"I know Nikki accused you of killing Al Cecchi. And now she's dead and, surprise, you're the one who found the body. So what are you trying to do by giving the cops background on me? You think that's going to get you off the hook?"

"I didn't kill Al," Simone said calmly. "I didn't kill Nikki. I simply had the bad luck to be in the wrong place at the wrong time."

"So *you* say."

"And so the authorities will prove when they come up with the real killers."

Or killer, singular, whichever the case might be. It was likely both Al and Nikki were victims of the same person.

Simone's heart pumped double time as she considered Sam Albright. What if he was the killer? What if she was his next intended victim?

"Let's get this straight, Sam. I didn't talk about you to the detectives in charge of the case. But a little research on their part would pull up your legal connection to Al Cecchi. Your arrest was a matter of record, after all." Seeing his face darkening at the reminder, Simone said, "You need to leave, Sam. *Now!*"

"I'm going. And you keep out of my business or you'll be sorry," he warned as he moved toward the door.

"You mean dead?" she asked, daring to put her fear into words.

He stopped short and faced her. "Take it any way you want, Simone. Keep in mind *dead* might not be the worse thing that can happen."

"What could be worse?"

"A person can be destroyed in many ways." Albright's grin was almost a leer when he said, "Something happening to one's kid, for example."

Simone gasped. Albright was threatening her with Drew! Nothing could make her angrier.

Without thinking, she said, "I would be careful if I were you, Sam. My brother wouldn't take kindly to anything happening to Drew or me."

"I'm supposed to be afraid of your brother?"

"If you aren't, you ought to be." Anger made her reckless. "Maybe you've heard of him—Michael De-Nali?"

The color drained from Albright's face, but his expression intensified. She'd used her brother's name—something she'd vowed never to do. Simone swallowed hard, but nothing in the world would make her take it back, not where Drew was involved. She would do anything to see that her child was safe.

Obviously understanding the threat, Albright walked out without another word, leaving Simone shaking.

She locked the door behind him, then checked the back door, as well. For the first time since she'd moved into this neighborhood, she didn't feel safe. Evil could strike anywhere, and tonight, she'd felt its presence.

Sam Albright had always seemed the most civilized of men, well-respected by his contemporaries…but apparently that was a veneer. Dark forces brewed beneath his carefully groomed surface.

Cass had said the identity of the murderer was "hidden"—could this be what she had meant—that it was the last person one would ever suspect?

If so, then Sam Albright went straight to the top of her list of suspects.

HEART POUNDING, he lunged out of the car. "Pop!"

The dark car pulled down the alley.

The license plate—RDN 1.

"Pop!" he cried, his voice breaking as he turned his father onto his back. He'd been shot in the gut and the chest. "Can you hear me? Please say you can hear me!"

His father's eyes opened and slowly focused. "Joey…"

"I'll get help, Pop, I'll get someone."

But his father gripped his wrist to stop him.

"DeNali…"

The first streaks of dawn lightened the sky when Gideon woke from the dream cursing. Why the hell had he replayed the memory again? The scenario revisited him nightly, as it had for months after the deadly event itself.

Back then, he'd tried avoiding the dream by avoiding sleep. He'd walked around too stunned to do more than acknowledge it. Eventually, the details had faded and then had slipped away. Now the dream was back, conjured, no doubt, by his renewed feelings for Simone. While he still mourned his father, he wasn't a kid anymore. He could face what had happened. That didn't mean he wanted to be haunted by the memory every night for the rest of his life!

If he could ever talk to someone about what had happened, it would be now. Not with Simone, though. He couldn't discuss what he'd seen with her. That would be like opening a wound and pouring in salt.

But he could talk to Cass.

Gideon never asked anyone for help. The very idea made him uncomfortable. But Cassandra Freed wasn't like other people. She had something extra—a developed sixth sense that she tried to hide. Maybe that was exactly what he needed to help him banish the nightmare for good.

Chapter Eleven

"I had an unexpected visitor when I arrived home last night," Simone told Gideon as they set off for their late-morning call on Galen O'Neill. She'd decided her imagination had been working overtime in her run down Clark Street, so she was keeping that to herself. "Sam Albright."

"What did he want?"

"To put the fear of God into me," she said, shuddering as she remembered the threat. "He figured I talked about the conversation that I overheard between him and Nikki. I never so much as mentioned his name to either of the detectives." She gave Gideon a searching look.

"If you're thinking one of my team did…" He shook his head.

"Not even Logan?"

"Logan would have told you first so you would be forewarned in case the information came back on you. Anyone could have overheard the threat that night, Simone. You just happened to be in Albright's line of sight."

"And now so is Drew."

Gideon jerked. "What do you mean?" he asked, his grip on the steering wheel becoming white-knuckled.

"Sam Albright threatened him. He said something happening to one's kid could be worse than death."

Gideon swore and she knew the reason Sam Albright had needed Al Cecchi's legal expertise in the first place was clear in his mind.

"I think it's time I met Sam Albright and we had a little chat."

"No! You'll be exposing yourself to trouble."

"Better me than Drew."

Appreciating the fact that he would put himself in jeopardy in order to protect their son, she said, "I made him think twice about his threat."

Without hesitating, Gideon murmured, "Michael."

Simone nodded. Still not proud of the fact, she nevertheless continued to believe her doing something so out of character—something she'd sworn only a few days ago she would never do—had been justified. Terrifying how life—and good intentions—could change so quickly.

The DePaul area wasn't far from where Gideon had picked her up, and just moments later they were on Galen's street, looking for parking, not a terrible feat at this time of day. Simone had called the auction chairwoman to make certain she would be home. She'd used the pretext of wanting to drop off some tear sheets of one of the society columns.

Red Carpet Christmas and the silent auction had

been featured…and so had been the murder. No way had the reporter been willing to forgo the juicy details.

Leaving the vehicle, Gideon and Simone approached the brick and limestone building whose door and first floor windows were decked out for the season in pine wreaths and red velvet ribbon. Gideon opened the black wrought iron gate for her and Simone slipped inside what she knew to be a landscaped garden area most of the year, though it was currently hidden under a foot of snow. It wasn't until she was down the walk and halfway up the stairs that she noticed the door and stopped dead.

"Uh-oh." Her breath caught in her throat and she choked out, "Door's open."

Gideon brushed into her before stopping. "You were expected," he offered.

But he didn't sound convincing.

Simone's heart banged against her ribs, and for once Gideon had nothing to do with it or her racing pulse. The scene reminiscent of her visit to Nikki Albright made her want to spin around and run away. But surely Galen was all right—surely she was simply suffering from frayed nerves.

When she knocked on the door and called inside, there was no answering greeting. All too familiar, indeed. Simone flashed Gideon a look of horror. This couldn't be happening to her again…

"Wait here." He gave her shoulders a quick squeeze before swinging the door open wide. "I'll go in."

"Should I call 911?" she asked, slipping the cell phone from her pocket.

Stopping in the doorway, he glanced back at her. "I'd rather be prepared. Let's find out what's up first."

The same mistake she'd made the day before.

Besides, was Gideon really prepared for what he might find? Thankful she and Cass hadn't run into the murderer the day before, Simone wondered if her luck could hold.

"But what if—"

Gideon cut her off, features hard. "Thanks for being worried, but I can take care of myself."

Certain he could—he was suddenly all alpha male, spine straight, nostrils flaring—she nevertheless watched him enter the house with her stomach knotting.

"Hel-lo," he quickly muttered.

"What?" Simone automatically stepped inside. Though Gideon was blocking her view, she saw a room that had been ripped apart…and an arm stretched across the living room floor. "Oh, no, not another…"

A moan from the body had Gideon stooping, feeling for a pulse. Simone rushed to his side.

"She's alive," he assured her.

"Thank God."

Remembering her cell phone, Simone put through the call for help. By the time she clicked the phone off, Galen was sitting up, her back against the couch, her fingers tentatively touching the side of her head. She moaned again.

"I'll get some ice," Simone said.

"No, wait," Gideon said. "Whoever did this could still be in the house. You stay with her and I'll get it."

Once more surprised by his protectiveness, Simone let Gideon have his way.

And then she settled to her knees and inspected Galen. For a woman who'd been knocked unconscious, Galen wasn't looking too bad. Her color was good and her eyes were in focus. From the odd expression that flitted across her features, her mind seemed to be working just fine.

"So what happened?" Simone asked.

"You tell me."

Simone started and backed off. "You think I had something to do with your being attacked?"

"How would I know? *I'm* the victim here."

Her saying it that way raised Simone's hackles. "We just got here, Galen. Your front door was open—"

"Like Nikki's! Dear Lord, I'm lucky to be alive." Galen shrank back slightly.

Simone told herself not to be insulted. Galen had been someone's victim—someone the woman hadn't seen. She'd been knocked out, so it was only natural that she would be confused and mistrustful.

Only…she didn't exactly seem confused.

Studying the other woman more closely, Simone said, "Gideon came into the house first and saw you on the floor. I was right behind him."

"Isn't he your alibi for Nikki's murder?"

The other woman's sly tone and expression were similar to what Simone had noted the morning before at the club's post fund-raiser meeting.

"I'm not liking where this conversation is going, Galen. Especially not when I don't have anything to hide." At least not related to murder. "But you do. I'm talking about Al Cecchi. Or should I call him Albert the way you do?"

Galen's complexion darkened, and her mouth opened and closed like a fish out of water. "I—I don't know what you're talking about."

"Sure you do. You were Al's mistress. The question is when? And for how long? And how did it end? I guess that's three questions. Sorry."

"You're delusional!"

Simone glimpsed Gideon hovering in the next room, zipped plastic bag of ice in hand, as she said, "Maybe the police won't think so."

"You can't tell them! You'll ruin me!"

"Then it's true."

"All right. It happened last year. It was simply a single indiscretion, not an affair. But if William found out about it, that would be the end of the marriage for me. Our prenup... I would be left with nothing. I'm too old to start over. Please, Simone."

Was Galen telling the truth? Simone didn't know her well enough to decide.

Gideon chose that moment to make himself known. "No sign of anyone here. This ice should bring down the swelling."

"Thank you."

Galen took the bag from him and placed it over a spot on the back of her head. Simone's eyebrows shot up. The woman had been nursing the side of her head when she'd first sat up.

"So what was the intruder looking for?" Gideon asked.

"How would I know? He didn't say anything."

"He? You know it was a man? You saw him, then?"

"No!" Galen insisted, looking around the room. "I saw nothing. He hit me and I was out."

Was Galen lying? Why? To protect herself? Hit her with what? Nothing lying around the area looked like a weapon.

Hearing the ambulance pull up outside, Simone decided to hold her peace for a while. "I won't say anything—"

"Thank you!"

Simone didn't have time to add "for now" before footsteps tromped up the outside stairs.

Paramedics were preceded by two uniformed officers. As Galen was being checked out for trauma, the male officer asked her questions about who might have broken in and why. Galen protested that she hadn't a clue. The female officer got the lowdown from Simone and Gideon, including the possibility of a connection to what happened at Nikki Albright's.

Which made Simone wonder about Galen and Sám. If Sam Albright was the connection between the first two murders, what would be his connection with Galen?

Not that she had the opportunity to ask.

Not that she *would,* at least not in front of the police. She didn't want Sam finding out that she was discussing him. If alerted to the fact, he might ignore her warning and come after Drew.

Once the officer jotted down sufficient notes about the break-in, she called them in, then went to take a look upstairs just as the paramedic finished checking out Galen.

"You're very lucky your friends were quick-thinking getting you that ice," the paramedic told Galen. "Not so much as a bump."

"Well, it hurts like there's one!" Galen argued, eyeing the male officer who'd stopped nearby.

Simone noticed she was holding the ice bag in a slightly different spot than she had been earlier.

Hmm…

"If you'll come with us, we'll take you to the closest emergency room."

"I can't leave now." Galen gestured to the mess around her. "I don't have a concussion, do I?"

"Not that I can tell."

"And I'm not bleeding."

"Not on the outside. We need to be sure you're all right, ma'am."

"But my home—"

"Will still be here when you get back," the officer said. "Perhaps you want to look around and see what might be missing before you go to the E.R."

"A doctor really should check her out first," argued the paramedic.

Simone knew they couldn't force anyone to go to the hospital. But surely anyone who'd really been hurt would be willing to be examined. Frustration crossed Galen's features, but in the end, she acquiesced, though she insisted on calling her husband to let him know what was going on.

And then, despite the paramedic's protests, she took a quick tour downstairs.

Circling back to where the others were waiting, she appeared puzzled. "I don't see anything missing."

Simone had noted that priceless works of art were still on the walls, a silver candelabra still on the fireplace. But as had been the case at Nikki's, couch cushions had been thrown around and drawers had been opened, papers everywhere, the media stand and bookcases emptied.

The officer who'd been inspecting the second floor descended, saying, "All kinds of expensive stuff lying around upstairs. Whoever did this must have been looking for something specific. You might as well go to the E.R., Mrs. O'Neill. We have to wait for the evidence technicians to arrive. One of us or a detective will catch up to you, either at the hospital or here. Should we need to vacate the place before you or your husband return, we'll lock up tight."

"Fine." Galen marched out the door, the paramedic following.

"Come on, let's go," Gideon said softly.

The male officer cleared his throat. "I've been asked to detain you two."

"You have no grounds for arrest," Gideon said.

At which the officer gave him a sharp look. "I didn't say anything about arrest."

"The detective in charge wants to talk to you," his partner said.

"We've told you all we know," Simone protested, feeling the walls of Galen's home closing in around her.

"Not my call, ma'am. I'm just following orders."

A few minutes later, the evidence technicians arrived and the officers wandered away, every so often shooting a glance at Simone and Gideon as if expecting them to make a run for it.

"Three strikes and I'm out," she muttered.

"You may get hassled, but they're not going to arrest you," Gideon assured her. "You were simply in the wrong place at the wrong time."

"Again!"

How could this keep happening to her? Simone wondered. At least she hadn't entered the house alone. Of course, a lot of good that had done her with Norelli yesterday. But in the end, he hadn't arrested her.

She simply had to believe her luck would hold.

It was mid-afternoon by the time they were able to catch some lunch at John Barleycorn's, a nearby bar and restaurant with what Simone claimed were the best burgers in town. The place was dark but inviting—old-fashioned carved wooden bar, pressed metal ceiling, myriad model ships lining the upper walls. Gideon knew he wasn't the best-spirited person on an empty stomach, so he waited until he'd wolfed down half a burger before broaching the subject.

"So what do Cecchi, the Albright woman and Galen O'Neill have in common?"

The detectives hadn't asked, undoubtedly because

they weren't in the loop yet. Because the O'Neill house was in a different part of the city than the other two crime scenes, the O'Neill case had gone to yet a third area office and a third set of detectives. Gideon was certain the police investigation would all get on board quickly, so he'd already put in a call to Logan to keep tabs on what was happening.

"In common? You mean, other than knowing me?" Simone shrugged and took a sip of her iced tea. "Al is the common denominator for the two women."

"There has to be something else. Remember the cop said the intruder must have been looking for something specific. This wasn't a simple burglary."

"Nikki's place was the same. It was a wreck. Obviously her murderer had been searching for something specific, because the valuables hadn't been carted away from there, either. If it was just a *thing* the person wanted, why murder anyone over it?"

Why had his own father been murdered? Gideon wondered.

Trying to keep his voice natural, he said, "Who knows what goes through the mind of a criminal."

"Galen wasn't murdered," Simone was saying.

"No, but she was knocked out. Nikki might have surprised whoever it was and then tried to fight the bastard," Gideon said, biting into his burger and washing it down with a slug of beer.

Simone picked at her food. She was silent for a moment before asking, "What about Al, though? He was killed at the party. No burglary involved there."

"Maybe the murderer thought he had something valuable on him."

"What would be valuable enough that someone would kill to get his hands on it?" Simone murmured.

"Evidence of a crime comes to mind. Cecchi was a criminal lawyer."

"But his job is to protect his clients."

"What if the murderer wasn't a client? What if a client gave him something that proved *someone else* committed a crime? He might have been planning on turning over evidence to clear his client."

"And the guilty one decided to stop him!" Simone said, sudden excitement fueling her so that her cheeks flushed becomingly.

Gideon stared. She was so vibrant, so determined to do what the average person would be happy to leave to the authorities. Or to someone she could hire. Simone could have left the case to him and his team, but she hadn't. Why? Because she didn't trust him to get the job done?

Or because she did?

Could it be that Simone wanted to be as close to him as he did to her?

Knowing that line of thinking had to wait—they had a lot in the past to sort out—he said, "Now we need to figure out why the murderer would think Nikki Albright or Galen O'Neill had whatever it was."

"Sam Albright has my vote."

"He obviously had a connection to both Cecchi and his ex-wife, but what connection did he have to Galen?

Besides which, he was Cecchi's client, which negates our speculation about the evidence."

"This is making my head hurt." Simone frowned. "Every time I think we're getting somewhere…" Then her expression changed. "I'm not so sure Galen's did."

Confused by her turnaround, Gideon asked, "What are you getting at?"

"When we first found her, Galen was holding the side of her head. Then when you brought her the ice pack, she put it at the back and later to yet another spot. The paramedic said she didn't have a concussion or even a lump. And she didn't want to go the emergency room. Remember, the paramedic pushed her into agreeing."

Gideon prided himself on being observant, but apparently he'd missed the stuff about the ice pack. "You don't think she was hurt."

"It just seemed…suspicious."

"As in her tearing up her own place and pretending she'd been attacked? What would be her point?"

"Galen knew I was going to be there," Simone reasoned. "What if she wanted everyone to believe she was a victim, too? Her fingerprints are on that dagger they took out of Al's chest, remember. She had a thing with Al and was worried that her husband would find out. Maybe he threatened to tell the man and she panicked."

"Okay. But then how does Nikki play into this?"

Simone made a sound of frustration and slumped back into her chair. She took a bite of her burger and chewed thoughtfully before excitedly gulping down some tea to help her swallow.

"The desk!" she gasped. "Why didn't we think of it before? Al and Nikki were fighting over the desk Teresa donated without his knowing. That kind of desk has a secret compartment. A convenient hiding place for something of value. That would explain why Al was so livid. Somehow, the murderer must have figured out Al's hiding place."

"The desk was in Nikki's living room," Gideon said. "But it was torn apart."

"So whatever was supposed to be in there was gone by the time the murderer searched it," Simone concluded.

They were of the same mind, Gideon thought. And he also realized they were finally getting somewhere.

He said, "Nikki might have found the object and removed it."

"Or not. Whatever it was might have been gone by the time the desk went up for auction. As auction chairwoman, Galen had private access to it, which would make her a target. Maybe she wasn't faking anything."

Gideon could see Simone getting frustrated again, but he was certain they were on to something. "Did anyone else have access to the desk?"

"Not that I know of. The delivery people, I guess, but they were simply hired, no one involved with Al. Then, again…I've been wondering why Josie Ralston was at the party. What if Al told her about the desk and she was there to check it out herself?"

"It would help if we knew what Cecchi hid in the damn thing."

"We can't ask him now, but we *can* ask Teresa," Simone said, her troubled expression gradually clearing. "At the wake tonight."

Chapter Twelve

The funeral home was all too familiar to Simone—it was where the wake for David had been held. That's all she could think about as she made polite conversation with acquaintances who'd come to pay their last respects to Al Cecchi.

The main room's fireplace was roaring, and the couches surrounding it were full. The heat was getting to her, but she'd been avoiding going into the parlor where Al was laid out—the same one that had been used for David. Eventually, she had to stop stalling and go inside. Alone.

If she chose to go to the funeral the morning after next, she would have to decide whether to take Drew with her. For tonight, thankfully, he'd already made plans to bunk at a friend's house for the night.

Not so thankfully, a last-minute crisis at the club had kept Gideon from meeting her. He'd said he would be late, but she'd been waiting for a while now. She had no idea of when—or if—he would arrive, and she was anxious to get some answers. She hated doing this alone, not because she was afraid, but because she hated not having Gideon at her side. She was starting to depend on him entirely too much. A few days of his helping her couldn't erase his betrayal.

Taking a deep breath, Simone entered Parlor A and quickly signed the guest book.

She swept her gaze around the spacious room with comfortable-looking seating areas with couches and chairs and low-lit lamps, just like in a real living room.

Michael stood in the line to speak to the widow. He, too, was alone—well, if she didn't count his shadow Ulf, who stood to the side, keeping watch on the room. No Josie. The woman had said she wasn't coming to Teresa's party, and it seemed she'd stuck to her word.

Thinking to join Michael, Simone quickly changed her mind. She wanted to speak to Teresa alone, not with her brother being within earshot. Whatever Al had hidden in the desk wasn't his business. It could wait.

She busied herself looking at the photographs the widow had brought. Family photos of Teresa and Al and their kids at various stages in their lives. She'd laid out similar photos of her and Drew and David for her husband's wake. Memories of their life together were already fading, a realization that made her panic inside. She wondered how much of an influence Gideon was in that respect. She didn't want to forget David, not ever, and Drew certainly wouldn't.

Although her head told her to keep things between

her and Gideon on a professional basis, she couldn't seem to put aside her feelings for him, which seemed to be as strong as they had been when she was in high school. They were unthinkable for her, given his testimony against her father; they were dangerous for Gideon. Michael always made good on his threats.

When she glanced up again, her brother was deep in conversation with Teresa, who was looking none too pleased. Her spine was ramrod stiff and her expression was definitely angry. And there was something else… fear?

What the heck was Michael saying to her?

Whatever it was, Michael kept it brief. He strolled away from the widow and to the coffin, where he paused to look down at the man inside. Then he turned away and, without glancing in Simone's direction, left the room, with Ulf trailing him as usual.

"How brave of you to attend Albert's wake, Simone," came a voice directly behind her.

Simone turned to find Galen O'Neill, appearing deceivingly frail but lovely in a pale gray dress.

"I could say the same of you."

If she had suffered any ill effects from her earlier trauma, it certainly wasn't evident.

"William would have wondered about it if I hadn't come," she said.

Simone glanced at the husband who was the cuckold—he stood a few yards away holding self-important court with several other men—and wondered how many secrets Galen withheld from him.

"You do remember our agreement," Galen said, keeping her voice down.

"I remember." Simone faced her squarely. "Depending on the circumstances, agreements can be amended."

Galen's nostrils flared and her eyes sparked before she spun on her heel and walked away, leaving Simone wondering what Galen was hiding.

Simone turned to see Teresa coming her way. Sam Albright intercepted her.

"Teresa, my dear, so sorry for your loss," Simone heard him say as he patted the widow's hand. He glanced up and locked gazes with Simone. "We've both lost someone dear to us, but if justice prevails, the murderer will pay."

Irritated that he was singling her out, Simone clenched her jaw into a stiff smile and stood firm.

"Tragic about poor Nikki," Teresa said. "It surprises me that you're here, Sam."

Had she forgotten that Nikki had divorced the man? Simone wondered.

"Yes, well, circumstances as they are, Nikki's sister has shut me out from making the arrangements or from being with family."

"At a time like this." Teresa was patting his hand now.

Simone thought she had never heard such a load of insincerity in her life. Albright aimed a sly smile her way, gave the widow a gentle hug and then found a new audience. Simone stared after him until she realized Teresa was in her space. For a new widow holding court at her husband's wake, she was looking exceedingly at ease. As had been the case the other night, no puffy eyes or swollen nose or blotchy skin indicated she'd been grieving.

And yet, Simone still thought she had been. Something about the glint deep in her eyes spoke to her. Everyone had his own way of dealing with death, she knew.

"Teresa, once more, may I offer my condolences," Simone said sincerely.

"Is that why you're here? I mean, you didn't get along with Al, at least not lately."

Simone let that go. There would plenty of time to pursue the money issue.

Instead, she said, "Why wouldn't I pay my respects? Al was my husband's partner for seventeen years."

"You mean Al carried your husband."

Simone was taken aback, unable to believe Teresa would say such a thing at her husband's wake. It raised all kinds of questions in her mind. The phrase *crime of passion* popped into Simone's head. Teresa knew Al had had mistresses; she'd punished him by putting the desk up for auction. Could she have killed him for it?

When she found her voice, Simone admitted, "David did learn a lot from Al. For that, I respected your husband. And no one should have to die the way he did. Do the police have any leads?"

"Other than you?"

"I didn't do it, Teresa. I think you know that."

"If they have anything, they haven't informed me."

"You knew him better than anyone. What about your gut feeling? Do you have any idea of *why* he was killed?"

Teresa stared right at her. "Not a clue."

Simone stared back, looking for the widow's reaction when she said, "I think he was killed over the desk."

"What?"

Teresa started. Was she really surprised that the desk might hold some clue…or simply surprised that Simone had guessed correctly.

"The desk you donated to the auction," Simone went on. "It had a secret compartment. I think Al hid something important and dangerous in it—possibly evidence of a crime. Something dangerous enough to be killed for."

Teresa's face crumpled and she appeared horrified. "No, that can't be."

"It seems as though Nikki was killed for whatever was inside, but apparently the object had already been removed before the murderer got to her place," Simone went on. "This morning, Galen's house was burglarized in the same manner, and it would be too much of a coincidence to think all three crimes *aren't* connected."

"I always hated that desk—what it represented," Teresa said, speaking more to herself than to Simone. "Albert's mother wasn't as saintly as he let on. I just wanted to hurt him the way he hurt me."

"So you gave away the desk and with it, whatever

Al hid in it. *That's* why he was so angry with you the night he died."

A single tear trickled down the widow's cheek. "So *I'm* responsible for Albert's death. And Nikki's. Oh, my God!"

Simone shifted uncomfortably. "I didn't say that. Whatever Al hid in the desk got him killed."

"If I hadn't been so angry at him…"

Teresa's guard was down. Simone could see that she was a hairbreadth away from bursting into tears.

"What could have been in the desk, Teresa?" Simone asked gently, hating that she'd brought new grief to the widow, but nonetheless needing answers. "Do you have any idea of what the murderer wanted to get from Al and Nikki and Galen?"

"I—I don't know."

"Think, Teresa, please," Simone urged her. "This could be important."

Teresa's uneasy gaze flicked upward from Simone's face to a point above her right shoulder. Simone turned to see Ulf standing within earshot. And nearby, Sam Albright was staring at her…had *he* heard their conversation, as well?

"Ulf, what is it?" Simone asked.

"Your brother would like to speak with you. He's in the car."

"Tell Michael I'll be there in a few minutes."

"He wants to speak to you *now*."

It seemed her brother's bodyguard wasn't going to back off. Irritated that she had been interrupted when she might have been getting somewhere with Teresa, Simone knew she'd lost her opportunity.

"Teresa," she murmured and moved off with Ulf.

Grabbing her coat from the closet, she slipped into it and shot outside. Her brother was in the back seat of the dark sedan parked across from the funeral home exit doors. Ulf stood sentry at the car. Apparently her brother wanted to speak to her alone.

She opened one of the rear doors and asked, "What is it, Michael?"

"Get in."

Even in the faint light of a streetlamp she could see he looked as grim as he sounded. What now? She slid in next to him and closed the door.

"I'm in. So what is so important?"

"I've heard some talk about you going around trying to catch Al Cecchi's murderer."

"Where would you hear a thing like that?" Simone kept her voice light, though she wasn't pleased that Michael knew anything about it.

"Where I heard it doesn't matter. Whether or not it's true does."

No doubt the information had come straight from Teresa. Had that been the subject of Michael's earlier discussion with the widow that had upset them both?

"I've just been asking a few questions—"

"Well, stop!"

"I have a vested interest in finding out the truth, Michael. I am still a suspect in Al's murder." Not to mention Nikki's, she was sure. Having done time herself, Cass would no doubt be discounted as her witness.

"And what's the deal with your doubling up with the owner of Club Undercover? What's his name?"

"Gideon," Simone said, her heart pounding. Surely Michael hadn't seen them together or he would know Gideon was really Joey Ruscetti, just as she had the moment she'd seen him. "He has an interest, too, since Al was murdered at his club."

"I don't like it. You're going to get hurt. What do you know about this guy?"

Which was it—he didn't like her working with Gideon, or her being with another man that he hadn't picked out for her? She couldn't forget Gideon's accusation that he'd bought David for her. David *had* loved her, she reminded herself.

"I know I can trust Gideon to watch my back." Despite the past, she did trust him, Simone thought, even above her own brother. What a perfect irony.

"I only want what's best for you, Simone."

"I know."

"You're everything to me—you and Drew. You're the only ones I can count on. The only constant in my life. I don't want to see anything bad happen to you."

"Ditto."

"Okay, then. If you need a murderer found so you're off the hook, leave it to me."

Simone stiffened. She wouldn't put it past Michael to invent a murderer just to clear her. "I can't let you do that, Michael."

He made a sound of exasperation and hit the steering wheel with the flat of his hand. "You are the most stubborn woman I've ever known."

"I thought your various wives had that honor," Simone said.

Michael snorted. "Don't remind me."

"You always think someone who disagrees with you is plain stubborn."

"All right, all right. Point taken. You're not going to stop."

That was too easy, Simone thought, as she said, "No, I'm not stopping."

"Then at least promise to be careful."

"Promise."

"Need a ride home?"

"I drove. But thanks."

"Get out of here. I have places to go. People to see."

"The woman from the party?" Simone asked, pretending not to know Josie's name.

"Nah, I'm over her."

"Already?"

"I took her to dinner and she was fishing around for a loan. I guess even society dames are looking out for their financial welfare."

Not that Josie was a society dame. Odd that she'd been at the party at all. Simone couldn't see Al wanting her there. Had she come to see her competition—Teresa—in person? Then what would have made her leave with another man?

Simone was still thinking about Josie as she drove

home, wondering if she knew more about Al's ship coming in than she'd let on. Again, she wondered why Josie had shown up at the fund-raiser. Had Al let something slip about the desk's hidden treasure and she'd come to check it out for herself?

Simone couldn't shake the idea that Josie Ralston knew something she hadn't told them.

GIDEON FELT AS IF his skin were too tight by the time Cass arrived at his office. Her glitzy red sweater reminded him of the upcoming holiday and of the fact that he would probably spend it alone again.

"Sorry, boss, but it got crazy out there. Mags couldn't handle the crowd alone."

Wanting to get this over with so he could leave the club and get over to the funeral home and Simone, he said, "Sit."

Logan had told him that if any more heat was put on the crimes, the FBI would step in as they often did when murders were connected. That was too reminiscent of his and Simone's past, and he hoped to clear her name as soon as possible.

Sliding into a chair opposite his desk, Cass gave him a curious look. "Is there a problem?"

"Personal. Mine."

"What can I do?"

"Help me put a nightmare to rest."

"Um, am I supposed to take this literally?"

"I'm afraid so. First, you have to promise me what we talk about will stay in this room."

"I swear."

Gideon had never voluntarily revealed any of this before, but not only did he trust Cass, he also hoped she could help him.

"My background is a little murky," he began. "My real name is Joseph Ruscetti and a couple of lifetimes ago, my father Frank Ruscetti was a Chicago Mob boss. I was a teenager when I witnessed his murder. Richard DeNali shot him in the alley behind our home."

Cass's eyes widened, telling him she knew who De-Nali was. "Gideon, I'm so sorry."

"Richard DeNali is Simone's father," Gideon told her.

"Oh, my God! I knew I sensed a strong connection between you two."

"The strongest," he admitted. Surely nothing was stronger than love…or so he had thought until Simone had cut him off. "Well, it was until my testimony helped put Simone's father in jail. She doesn't believe he did it. I had a nightmare about what I saw every night for months afterward until I managed to push it away. Since Simone came back into my life, every night I'm replaying my father's murder in my dreams again."

"That must be horrible for you. What can I do?"

"Help me get the damn nightmare out of my head."

Cass's forehead pulled into a frown. "We have dreams for reasons."

"But not the same one over and over."

"Who says? The subconscious is tricky. It sounds like yours is trying to tell you something."

"Yeah, that Simone and I don't stand a chance together."

"Maybe."

"What else could it be? You're psychic. Can't you figure it out?"

Cass fidgeted in her chair as she usually did when the psychic business surfaced. "It's not my nightmare, Gideon. They're not my emotions. Besides, this psychic business isn't all it's cracked up to be. You know I don't see things literally."

"Can't you try?"

Reluctantly, Cass said, "All right. I'll try if you will."

"What do we do?"

"One way of dealing with a bad dream is to take it out and inspect it when you're awake. Examine it. Take it apart. Close your eyes and replay it like a movie in your mind."

Nodding, Gideon closed his eyes and concentrated on that night seventeen years ago. He saw the car. The men. The glint of light on the visitor's glasses. The blue flash. The license plate. His pulse accelerated as he reexamined each second of the horrific scene.

Nothing new came to him.

Finally, he opened his eyes and shook his head. "Nothing. It's all the same."

Cass's gaze was troubled. "You're not really certain of that. Deep inside, you're afraid."

"Of what?"

"I can't give you any answers, Gideon, I'm sorry. You have to do that for yourself. Examine the nightmare from different angles. Stop hanging back. Get close to it. Give it a different ending if you have to."

"A different ending…" How he wished. "Pop still alive…that would change everything."

"But he is alive in your heart, isn't he?" Cass asked.

"Maybe that's what this is all about. Pop haunting me because I've gotten involved with his killer's daughter again." Like he'd said, maybe he was supposed to figure out that he and Simone weren't meant to be together. "Thanks, Cass. I'll work on it."

In the meantime, he needed to get over to the funeral home—Simone was no doubt wondering what had happened to him.

He couldn't believe they'd been brought back together by such unusual circumstances only to be ripped apart once more. Fate couldn't be that cruel—taking Simone from him twice and now a son, as well. Somehow this whole thing had to work out. He had to make it work out…

Arriving at the funeral home in record time, he scanned the lot for Simone's car but didn't see it. She wasn't in the open area of the funeral home, either, so he entered the parlor where Al Cecchi's wake was being held and stopped at the guest book to see if she'd signed in. Her name was high on the list—she'd arrived early. About to set off to look for her, he stopped cold when his gaze hit another familiar name.

Anthony Viglio.

Someone's idea of a joke? Who would sign a dead man's name? Or was the dead man in fact alive?

Gideon gazed around the room as if the man in question would present himself. If there was a thug in the room, he couldn't spot the guy—no one stood out. Not that he knew Viglio was a thug. He could be a perfectly respectable businessman. Rather he could *look* like one. No one who had to pay a criminal lawyer half a mil could be considered respectable…assuming he really was alive.

Gideon refocused and moved through the crowded room trying to find Simone. Instead, he nearly ran into Teresa Cecchi.

"What are you doing here?" she demanded.

"Paying my respects. Your husband was killed in my establishment. My condolences for your loss."

The widow nodded. "I'm surprised you and Simone came separately."

"Actually, I promised to meet her here."

"You missed her."

"How long ago did she leave?"

"About half an hour ago. Her brother's bodyguard interrupted us to say Michael wanted to speak to her."

"Michael was here?" Although that stood to reason, considering Simone's brother had funded Cecchi and Burke.

"You know Michael DeNali?"

Gideon hedged the truth, saying, "Not really, but Simone has spoken of him. So she left and didn't come back?"

"I didn't see her again."

Assuming Simone had headed for home, Gideon

made his excuses and left. Once on the road driving north, he pulled out his cell and called hers. When it connected, it sent him directly to her voice mail. He was no more successful in trying to reach her at home.

Why wasn't she answering?

And why hadn't she waited for him? Had she learned something new?

Worried, he drove straight to her place. She'd told him Drew was studying with a friend, so he didn't have to worry about his son spotting him.

The house was dark. He double-parked and walked around to the back. No lights in the kitchen, either. He checked the garage—her car was inside. No answer when he rang the bell.

So where the hell was Simone?

Chapter Thirteen

As the elevator took her up to Josie Ralston's pent-house, Simone took a couple of steadying breaths. Thankfully, Gabe's friend, the guard, had been on duty and had recognized her from the last visit.

The doors whooshed open and her pulse fluttered as she stepped out and heard Christmas music echoing down the hall. A couple of steps took her to Josie's door, where Simone stopped short.

No, no, no. This couldn't be happening again.

The damn thing wasn't shut!

Light slashing through the door's opening crack and Christmas music invited her in. Simone's heart thudded and the flutter of her pulse accelerated.

Though her mouth had gone dry, somehow she called out, "Josie?"

No answer.

Had she really expected one?

Simone couldn't help herself. She reached out and pushed the door inward. The mess that met her gaze was no big surprise. Furniture overturned. Drawers torn out of their cabinets. Papers scattered everywhere.

All too familiar...

"Josie?" she called louder, though she figured she was talking to herself.

At least there was no body...well, not in the living area. She hadn't meant to enter another crime scene... not until she heard a soft cry from another room.

Then she didn't know what to do.

There was a crash and another cry.

Was it Josie stumbling around, hurt?

Cursing to herself, Simone couldn't leave. She stepped inside and headed in the direction of the sound, grabbing a makeshift weapon—a small sculpture that was far heavier than she'd imagined—on the way.

"Josie, where are you?"

Simone was halfway to the bedroom doorway when she glanced into the living area. She barely caught a reflection in a large mirror—something big and red—when the lights went out. Taking a breath was nearly impossible; she had to concentrate to pull air into her lungs.

Her heart thudded against her ribs and she remained frozen until she heard footsteps to her right. Then she turned and ran as fast as she could for the front door. It stood open, the low-lit hallway beyond her goal, but she heard the intruder directly behind her, felt a grasping hand catch her coat.

Turning, she swung out with the sculpture and connected without seeing where. But the hand released her.

A grunt of pain assured her she'd done damage and spurred her out the door. She hit the elevator button, but the stumbling sounds on the other side of Josie's door told her she didn't have time to wait for the doors to open.

Spotting the Emergency Exit sign at the end of the hall, she ran for the stairwell.

As she descended one…two…three steps at a time, her boots clunked against the cement stairs, making a racket that reverberated around her. Unable to tell whether that was another set of footsteps above her or an echo of her own, she kept going without so much as a glance back.

Nothing would slow her, not even the pain in her side or the lack of air reaching her lungs. At first, she kept count of floors, but they quickly became a blur. She practically flew down to the big red Exit sign indicating she'd reached the first floor.

With a cry of relief, she threw open the door and ran straight into a human wall.

"Ah!" she gasped, wailing against the person trying to hold her.

"Simone, what the hell?"

The familiar voice broke through her panic and she felt her knees give way.

Gideon caught her and swung her up into his arms and carried her over to the security guard station. Her chest was heaving; every breath was painful. Blood was pumping through her so fast she could feel its rush.

But Gideon was here now. She was safe. He wouldn't let anyone hurt her...

"Somehow I knew I would find you here," he said, setting her down on one of two lobby chairs.

"Josie's apartment," she gasped out. "Ransacked. He was still there, though."

"The intruder?" Gideon asked.

She nodded.

"You saw him?" asked the security guard, who'd left his desk.

"Mirror." The big red image came back to her. "Santa Claus."

Her mind racing, she filled Gideon and the security guard—Gabe's friend—in on the latest burglary. He told them to stay put and, unsnapping his gun holster, took an elevator up to investigate.

"You shouldn't have come here alone," Gideon said.

"I thought Josie might know something about Al's secret cache. Obviously, so did the killer."

"I told you I was going to be late, not that I was abandoning you. Why didn't you wait for me?"

"I didn't want to go back inside."

"You could have been hurt," he said, voice low, raising goose bumps on her skin.

He cared, she realized. Gideon cared about her. Warmth flushed through her. And confusion. She shouldn't care that he cared, but she did. She might have shut him out of her life, might have repressed the old feelings, but they reminded her they were there every chance they got.

Before the silence between them could become awkward, the security guard returned.

"No one up there now," he said. "I don't know how the bastard got in, but there wasn't any damage to the door. It wasn't a forced entry. No sign of the Ralston woman, either. Either she was already out or she got out. Now the two of you get out while the going is good. The cops don't need to know you were here. I can handle it."

It didn't take a second invitation. Gideon hustled her from the building, saying, "Gabe will be in touch," and steered her into the car he'd left in the drive.

It didn't take Simone long to realize he wasn't taking her home—he passed her street without so much as slowing.

"Where are we going?"

"My place. I want to talk and don't want to be interrupted."

Simone didn't argue. She didn't want to be alone, and Drew wouldn't be home.

It wasn't until they were in Gideon's place and she was feeling better sipping a brandy and warmed by the heat of a wood-burning fire, that Gideon said, "Santa Claus, huh?"

"I just had a glimpse—but I swear."

"You and the kid outside the Albright woman's place."

They were on the same wavelength, Simone thought, her back against several floor pillows directly in front of the fireplace. "Like I said, people underestimate kids." She hesitated only for a second before adding, "Um, Gideon, there's something else. After talking to Josie, I had the feeling someone was following me."

"Why didn't you say something?"

"Because I thought I was just on edge. I heard footsteps behind me and couldn't see anyone. But I went faster and so did the footsteps."

"But nothing happened?"

"I got jarred by the guy going past me, that's all. And then I started feeling foolish."

"So what's your point?"

"The guy who jarred me—he was wearing a Santa Claus suit."

The oath that flew from Gideon's mouth made Simone cringe.

"Why don't women trust their instincts?" he demanded.

"Well, I did run," she said faintly. "And I made sure I didn't walk home alone."

Gideon was silent for the moment it took to finish his drink and refill it. "The intruder at Cecchi and Burke—remember I said I couldn't grab onto the person. He was probably wearing a Santa suit then."

A thrill shot through Simone. "Or she."

"You really think it could have been Galen?"

Simone thought about it for a moment, then shook her head. "I don't know. I just got that quick glimpse before the lights went out."

"So all we have to do is find someone committing criminal acts while wearing a Santa suit."

The irony didn't escape her. "That'll be a piece of cake at this time of year."

She took another sip of the brandy and stretched her toes toward the fire. The setting was so intimate, almost as if they were on a date. Gideon was sitting on the rug, too, close enough that he could reach out and…

"What if it's Anthony Viglio?" he suddenly asked.

"But Viglio's dead."

"Then someone has a sick sense of humor—I found his name in the guest register at the funeral parlor."

Simone started. "Weird," she murmured, finishing her drink. "Anthony Viglio. I still haven't been able to place where I heard the name. I wonder if he could have been David's client at some time."

"Didn't the records indicate he was a *new* client?"

"New to Al. Who knows if all the records are in order? I should be able to find out, though. Rebecca would know."

"Rebecca?"

"Rebecca Finley, the office manager. She's been with the firm from the beginning. I'll talk to her tomorrow. See if I can figure out whether the phantom account had anything to do with what Al hid. If it was evidence…"

"What?"

"The money in Viglio's account could be blackmail money. What if Al was blackmailing Viglio?"

"Blackmail. Hmm. Because he's still alive? Putting Viglio's name on the account would kind of defeat the purpose of his playing dead."

Simone sighed. "Will we ever figure it out?"

"From now on, you ought to stay out of it."

"I can't stay out of it when I'm a suspect."

"I mean the investigation part. Talk to your office manager, but leave the rest to me."

"Where is this coming from?"

"I thought that would be obvious. You put yourself in danger tonight. And now I learn someone followed you the other night, as well."

"But I'm fine." Though she had been scared to death, and her pulse jumped just thinking about her close call.

"Next time you might not be so lucky. I don't want anything to happen to you, Simone."

She couldn't keep herself from saying, "That sounds like more than friendly concern."

"What if it is?"

There it was. The question she couldn't answer. Her father was rotting in jail because of him. And yet...

"What is it exactly?" she asked.

"My feelings for you haven't changed, Simone. You're the only woman who's ever had a piece of my heart."

"Just a piece?"

"There's room for negotiation."

He brushed the hair from the side of her face. Simone shuddered and felt herself unfurl inside. She'd locked the past up tight for so long. But this wasn't the past; this was the present. He wasn't Joseph Ruscetti, Mob boss's son. Gideon was a man in his own right. He'd navigated tough waters alone to become the person he was. The person who could forget past hurts to help a woman whose life was about to be destroyed.

And for that, she opened up to him. "Oh, Gideon, I need you."

"Simone…"

Her name swept past his lips right before they covered hers. Desire filled her and she opened to him, wrapped her arms around his neck, welcomed the feel of him against her. No protest escaped her when he pressed her down and swept his hand up under her sweater.

His touch was as familiar as if she'd felt it yesterday. She remembered everything—the way he touched her breast so lightly that it made her skin prickle, the way he circled her nipple with his thumb until it peaked and sent waves of pleasure through her.

Sensations flooded her and she was caught between tears and a growing passion that swept through her as it had all those years ago. She'd given in to her desire for him then, but she'd been young and in love.

She might not be young any more, but despite all reason, that all-consuming love swept through her once more.

Knowing that she couldn't have Gideon in her life, not without destroying Drew, Simone realized that this might be the one time they could be together. There might not be another opportunity.

Drawn together in danger…so formidable…so compelling.

"Simone," he groaned against her mouth, "if you want to stop, do it now."

"Don't stop."

The words were out of her mouth before she could consider them. Truth be told, she did want him, had never stopped wanting him. She couldn't resist just one more taste of him, even if it were all she would ever have.

For a moment, guilt flooded her.

David...

David had known he didn't have her whole heart. David would want her to be as happy as he'd made her during their life together. David was gone now, had been for some time, and Gideon was here.

And oh, how she wanted him.

For the moment, nothing else mattered. He'd proven himself to her by trying to clear her name, by staying true to his promise that he wouldn't reveal his identity to their son; surely that was enough.

Desire flooded her as he removed her sweater and pants, kissing sensitive flesh as he exposed it. She tugged at his clothes, and he helped her remove them. Soon they were naked in each other's arms, and for her, the moment felt so right.

Firelight flickered across his seductive flesh. Warmth spread and multiplied as he entered her. She watched his face—the passion, the pleasure he was feeling—because it excited her almost as much as the things he was doing to her body.

He kissed her again and rolled closer to the fire, leaving her on top. Heat flushed through her as she rode him. He cupped her breasts and squeezed until she gasped. Then he sent one hand trailing down her belly to their juncture. When he found her, the sensation was so piercing that she rode the crest and came with a cry.

A cry that was followed by his.

They froze for a moment before he took her face in both hands and brought it to his for a passion-filled kiss. Then, still inside her, he wrapped his arms around her back and drew her down against him until her world floated away.

HE SWIPED THE INSIDE of the foggy windshield. Pop and a man in an overcoat and brimmed hat. The man turned his head slightly and his dark-framed glasses caught the light.

Richard DeNali...what was Simone's father doing here?

Before he could get out of the car, a blue flash froze him to his seat. Another flash. No sound. His father fell into the snow and DeNali lit his cigarette one-handed before getting into his vehicle.

Heart pounding, he threw open the door and lunged out as the dark car pulled away. The license plate—RDN 1.

"Pop!" he cried, turning his father onto his back. "Can you hear me? Please say you can hear me!"

His father's eyes opened and slowly focused. "De-Nali..."

Gideon awakened, freaked out by the dream as if it were some evil portent.

What was he missing?

The dream was nagging him for a reason. It was there, had to be. He just had to figure out what, then take it out and examine it as Cass had suggested.

Before he could do so, Simone stirred next to him and, opening her eyes, uttered a shocked "Oh!"

"Didn't expect to see me?" he teased, her slightest movement inching up his hard-on. "You're at my place, remember."

Simone's confusion cleared and conflicting emotions quickly flitted across her beautiful face. Gideon's heart fell as fast as his erection. She couldn't even make love to him one night without regret.

Frantically, she grabbed her clothing and started dressing. "We can't do this again."

"Can't?"

"It was a mistake."

He reached out and stopped her from slipping the sweater over her head. "No."

"Let me!" She jerked her arm from his hand and pulled on the sweater. "I have to go home."

Gideon was already pulling on his underwear. "Whoa. Slow down. You've got a lead on me."

"Don't bother getting dressed. I'll take a taxi."

"You did that last time. This time, I'll make sure you get safely inside your house." Unable to miss her mulish expression, he said, "It's the middle of the night, so don't try to talk me out of it. You're not leaving without me."

She finished dressing fast, he finished faster, so he was ready to go out the door with her.

With each second, his anger built. He couldn't believe they'd come so far only to have her put on the brakes.

How could she be so cold?

Had it taken her long to learn to be like this? Did she really think he would go along with this sudden change of heart? That he would simply let her walk back out of his life as she had seventeen years ago?

The thought stunned him. No doubt that's exactly what she planned to do.

SIMONE FELT TENSION ooze from a silent Gideon nearly all the way to her place.

He was turning onto her block before asking, "Why is it so easy for you, I wonder?"

"Easy?" There was nothing easy about loving him.

"Leaving me," he said. "You were doing it again, weren't you?"

"I was simply trying to go home."

"Without so much as smile or a soft word or a kiss? We made love, Simone."

"We had sex." She needed to put an impersonal spin on it for her own peace of mind. "Don't confuse the two."

The moment she'd awakened, head clear, her doubts about him—*about them*—had resurfaced. And hadn't she already decided making love to him was going to be a one-time thing?

Gideon double-parked in front of her house. She unbuckled her seat belt and opened the door. "Thanks for the ride."

"I said I would see you inside."

Chilled by his cool, deliberate tone, she hurried up the walk ahead of him, but he caught up to her as she opened the door; when she stepped inside, he followed. She blinked up at him, her insides roiling with emotions. But she had learned to cover what she didn't want someone else to know.

"I'm in. I'm safe."

Gideon glared at her. "What happened, Simone? At least you can be honest about it."

"Can I really be honest with you, Gideon? All right. The past is always going to be between us."

That was the truth, as much as she hated it. She'd thought all the other good things about him could erase the past, but the first thing that had come to her when she'd opened her eyes was that she'd slept with the man who'd put her father behind bars for life.

"I thought we were beyond that," he said.

"We'll never be beyond that unless you wave some magic wand and make it all go away. I figure the odds are against that happening. And then there's…"

She was going to say *Drew* until she spotted his book bag next to the couch. He hadn't stayed the night at his friend's house, after all. Knowing he was in the house unsettled her. She didn't want father and son coming face-to-face.

"Then there's what?" Gideon asked.

"What does it matter. You need to go."

"You need to stop holding something that happened seventeen years ago against me."

"How can I when Papa is still in prison?"

"I saw him kill my own father. Should I have lied to the authorities to please you?"

Simone heard a noise. Pulse jumping, she checked the stairs, but saw nothing. Drew never stayed up this late. He was asleep and she was hearing things. Even so, she didn't want to take any chances.

"Good night, Gideon." She held the door open for him and indicated he should leave.

"We're not done, Simone."

He pulled her to him so fast she couldn't think. His kiss was angry. And short.

Then he was out the door.

Heat flushed through her as she locked the door behind him and then leaned against it for a moment. Flashes of their lovemaking flitted through her mind until she heard a low murmur overhead.

Drew...

As Simone rushed up the stairs, she heard his voice, purposely low. By the time she got to the landing and glanced into his room, he was hanging up the phone. Whom had he been talking to at this hour? He never left the door open when going to bed, so he'd obviously heard her downstairs and had come to see what was what.

Nerves taut, she said, "Drew, honey, I didn't think you were going to be home tonight."

"Change of plans, Mom. G'night."

Before she could ask what happened, he closed the door in her face.

Simone stood staring at the wood panel, wondering how much he'd overheard.

Chapter Fourteen

By the time Simone got up the next morning—she'd
overslept—Drew had already left for school. If he'd
eaten breakfast, she couldn't tell. That didn't upset her.
What upset her was that he hadn't told her he was leaving.

So unlike her overprotective son.

Certain that he'd been on the stairs when she'd been
talking to Gideon, she again wondered what Drew had
overheard.

Knowing she was going to have to deal with it later,
Simone tried to put that particular worry out of mind
as she started a pot of coffee, then headed back upstairs.
Even as vague as she was feeling, she realized the living room was a mess—what had Drew been doing this
morning? Surely if the place had looked like this when
she'd come home last night, she would have noticed.

Guiltily wondering if her son had been taking out his
frustration at whatever he had heard on the living room,
Simone rushed upstairs to shower.

She dressed in a forest-green pantsuit appropriate for an office. Cecchi and Burke Law Offices, to be exact. On the trail of the elusive Anthony Viglio, she meant to learn what she could about the phantom account.

Not wanting to arrive during the lunch hour and possibly miss the office manager, Simone grabbed a muffin and ate it with a quick cup of coffee.

Leaving the back way, she locked up even as thoughts of Gideon plagued her. No matter what her head said, her heart said once was not enough. That parting kiss had convinced her of that. Even loyalty to her father hadn't kept her from falling under Gideon's spell again.

Torn about what was ahead of her, Simone was distracted as she opened the door into the dark garage. Then a scrabbling noise made her heart thud. A rear car door stood open and a foot stuck out from the back seat.

"Hey, what do you think you're doing?" she yelled.

A mumbled oath blasted from the car and the person inside nearly exploded out of the vehicle in a flurry of brilliant color.

"Santa Claus!" she yelped as the padded figure plowed into her, knocking her over.

The red-coated figure came at her with a piece of rope in hand.

To strangle her like he had Nikki?

Light-headed, Simone struck out with a booted foot as hard as she could. Contact. The hand exploded upward, the rope went flying.

Santa came for her again, but she was already scrambling back. A gloved hand caught her foot and pulled so that she fell flat on her back, knocking the air out of her. She groped along the garage floor and found something hard and round—a piece of pipe. She struck out with the pipe and made contact, but Santa was padded and therefore protected.

But when the pipe was switched to Santa's hand and was raised over her, that was a different matter.

Thinking fast, Simone found her key ring and pressed one of the buttons on the pad so that the car alarm sounded and the lights flashed. Santa started and dropped the pipe. The sound blasting through the building was so loud it hurt her ears. Her attacker didn't waste any time in jumping over her sprawled body and taking off out of the garage.

Simone was on her feet in seconds and, without thinking, ran after the fleeing figure. But by the time she got to the alley, there was no sign of her attacker. No sign of a vehicle she could identify.

Chest heaving, pulse pounding as she caught her breath, Simone stood staring for a moment.

No wonder her place was such a mess. The person in the Santa suit—the murderer, she presumed—had gotten inside, undoubtedly the same way she and Gideon had gotten into Al Cecchi's private office. Thankfully, Drew had already left for school.

This time when she went into the garage, she turned on the overhead light. The rear door was still open. What had the bastard been doing in her car?

Looking inside, she felt a moment's confusion. The

box that held her music was open and the tapes and CDs were dumped everywhere. Santa was a music freak? Furthermore, the tapes were out of their boxes, as if Santa had been trying to make sure the right tape was in the right box.

Then it came to her.

A tape.

Maybe the killer was looking for a tape.

Now the only question was—of what?

"No more investigating on your own, is that clear?" Detective Norelli growled at Simone after taking her story.

"I'm simply looking out for my own interests. I don't want to spend time behind bars."

"Better than being dead."

"So you say."

He shook his head. "I'm done here for now, but you'll be hearing from me."

Simone hadn't admitted to being at Josie Ralston's place the night before, but she had told him how she had come to believe that the killer was trying to find a tape that could incriminate him in a crime. She was sure now that it was a man, because Santa had been too big and strong to be a woman. Well, at least not one Galen's size—not that she'd mentioned that conclusion to Norelli.

What she had suggested was that the tape had been hidden in the desk that had passed through multiple hands—the reason why various members of the club had been attacked, their homes searched.

Norelli had listened to her theory without comment. He'd taken enough notes, but if he was impressed with her logic, he didn't let on.

"What about them?" she asked of the evidence technicians.

There were two men. One had started in the garage, the other in the house. Now they were both taking prints in the living room.

"They're almost done," Norelli said. "Don't worry, you'll be able to clean up soon."

How long would that take? Simone wondered, itching to get to Cecchi and Burke.

"Here's my card. You get anything, use it."

Certainly a different attitude than he'd had the last time they'd met and he'd tried to pin Nikki's murder on her. Simone took the card and saw Norelli to the front door. Then she went upstairs and changed into jeans and a sweatshirt. By the time she got back to the living room, the two men were on their way out.

And then she was alone.

Simone told herself that being alone would be safe enough. That Santa had already been through her things and would have no reason to come back. She had to believe that or she would go out of her mind.

Cleaning up the mess in the living room, she thought about calling Gideon to let him know what was up. They hadn't parted on good terms the night before, so she kept her hands off the phone. If he knew, he would undoubtedly rush over here, and she wasn't ready to face him yet. She needed some breathing room. Time to think.

What was she going to do about him?

By the time she was done cleaning, she was no clearer on the Gideon problem than she had been when she'd started, so she put off calling him.

It was late afternoon before she arrived at Cecchi and Burke Law Offices. After exchanging pleasantries with the receptionist, a young law student named Penny who was new to the firm, she went directly to Rebecca Finley's office.

"Simone. What a surprise."

Rebecca removed her reading glasses and slid them out of sight on her desk. She might be on the verge of middle age, but she was attractive and a bit on the vain side. As usual, she wore a designer suit, this one of pink and cream bouclé.

"You're not shocked to see me, I hope."

"Considering that both partners are gone, I figured you would be around eventually."

"Actually, that's not why I'm here. Not exactly." Simone took the chair opposite the office manager's. "This may have something to do with Al's murder."

Rebecca couldn't hide her surprise. "I've told the police everything I know. The other lawyers and the rest of the staff, as well."

"Did you know Anthony Viglio?"

"Viglio?"

"A client."

"Yes, I know the name. How could I forget it when he's got a huge retainer on the books?"

Simone noted the way Rebecca had phrased it. *On*

the books. Not that there was any actual money to be had now.

"Was there anything unusual about the retainer?"

"Other than the amount? You bet. He paid in cash. Who walks around with a half a million in cash?"

Simone's heart beat faster. She was getting closer to the truth; she could sense it.

"You said you know the name. Not the client?"

"I've never met him. I'm not sure he's ever been here. If Al took an appointment with Viglio here, it wasn't on the calendar."

"What about on the phone?"

"Nope. Never spoke to him."

Feeling deflated, Simone asked, "Could he have come in while you were out?"

"Let's find out."

Though they checked with the associates and staff, no one seemed to have seen the man. Which pretty much meant he really was dead.

As she was leaving, the receptionist said, "Um, you were asking about Anthony Viglio…"

"You know who I'm talking about?"

"He was only here once, but yeah."

So he had been here! Or had he? "What did he look like, Penny?"

"Gorgeous for a criminal type," she said, as if she thought all criminals should be unattractive. "Big and blond and blue-eyed."

"Age?"

Penny shrugged her shoulders. "A lot older than me."

Which probably meant over thirty, Simone thought. "Anything unusual about him?"

Penny shook her head. "I didn't see him long enough to get a close look. Al took him into his office right away. And when Viglio left, he headed straight out the door without so much as looking my way."

"Like he was angry?"

"Yeah. Could have been."

"And you never saw or heard from him again?"

"Just that once."

Simone thanked the receptionist and left the offices.

Driving home in the dark, she thought about the discrepancy between this description and the photo Logan had printed out from the online obituary.

Anthony Viglio had been short and dark. A small man. So who had stolen his identity?

Big and blond and blue-eyed. Two men who fit that description came to mind—Sam Albright, Nikki's ex-husband, and Ulf Nachtmann, Michael's bodyguard.

Either one could be a killer.

AFTER PLACING several calls to Simone and getting her voice mail, Gideon decided to pay her another surprise visit. Though things had been awkward between them when they'd parted the night before, surely she'd had enough time to come around.

He knew she loved him as much as he did her.

But was that enough?

Double-parking the car in front of her house, he

noted only a single light on, as if no one were home. He ran up to the door and rang the bell. No answer. Just to make sure, he went around to the back. The lights in the kitchen were off, the garage was open and Simone's car was gone.

Cursing, Gideon ran back to the street just as some impatient dolt started laying on the horn. There was plenty of room to go around him, but obviously the guy couldn't handle his SUV on a city side street.

So where was Simone? he wondered as he pulled away from her house and into an empty area near a fireplug. The only thing he knew she'd planned for the day was a visit to Cecchi and Burke, but surely that hadn't kept her this long. He might as well leave, get over to the club and try to get some paperwork done. Who knew when she'd be home?

Heading for Clark Street, he checked his rearview mirror to see a dark vehicle pull out of a spot, catch up to him fast and make the turn with him.

His thoughts about Simone confused him. He'd meant to have it out with her, to make her admit their being together had meant something.

Brights behind him made him turn his rearview mirror to night vision. Idiot! Why in the world did anyone need brights on a well-lit city street?

Thinking he didn't want to go back to the club just yet, Gideon decided to take a spin on the Drive. He always did his best thinking at high speed.

He turned east on Fullerton and the brights turned with him—he caught the glare in his sideview mirror.

He sped up, but the brights stayed pinned to his mirrors.

Surely the other driver would turn off and head through the park, Gideon hoped. Only he didn't, and the damn brights grew annoying. Hoping to make the other driver anxious enough to go around him, Gideon slowed.

The brights stayed right in his mirrors.

An odd feeling, like fingers crawling up his spine, warned Gideon that he was being followed. So when he passed the zoo and approached Lake Shore Drive, he did so in the left lane with his left turn signal on.

And watched the left turn signal blink on behind him.

At the last minute, his pulse charged, Gideon swung across the right lane and entered The Drive going south rather than north.

The dark vehicle followed.

One of the many jobs he'd had in his bizarre life was at a car track. He'd driven the hot cars every chance he'd had. Thinking fast, he burned rubber only to have the dark vehicle stay with him. Suddenly it was coming alongside him, squeezing him to the embankment. Gideon dropped back, but not before the other vehicle popped him, jerking him in his seat.

Gideon saw red. This was no accident. This car had been following him from Simone's place.

When the other vehicle dropped back as if to begin another attack, Gideon floored the accelerator and didn't let up until he reached the next exit, where he sped off and veered back along the south end of Lincoln Park.

He wasn't alone.

Cornering this guy without ending up in a crash—that was the goal.

Thankfully, traffic was light. Gideon swung around the curve. The other vehicle swung wide and came up for another attack, no doubt intending to roll him into the park. Gideon acted first, hauling the wheel around so he rammed the other vehicle good. Then at the next intersection, he swung right again onto the main artery that cut through the park.

As Gideon passed the pond and café, he watched for the service road that used to be a throughway for visitors' cars. He took it and sped along the iron fence separating the zoo from the rest of the park.

Halfway to the parking lot on the east side, he saw the now familiar lights behind him.

Gideon grinned, shot forward and made another right. He was going to see who this bastard was. He drove as far as the stone tunnel to the pond and its service road, made the turn and another to the right and cut his lights.

Spun the car around.

Stopped.

Waited, engine purring, blood rushing through him as he set his trap.

The dark vehicle came to a screeching halt just before it ran into the pond. And Gideon flicked on his brights, illuminating the black sedan, which suddenly rolled in reverse back under the stone arch.

Now Gideon was following.

He hadn't gotten a good enough look at the vehicle or at the bastard driving it, but he wasn't about to give up until he knew who was after him and why.

The best laid plans often go awry…especially when the police were involved. A patrol car shot out of nowhere, blue lights blazing, and flashed a spotlight on Gideon.

Caught!

Regretfully, he watched the dark car speed away without ever having seen the driver.

"DREW, WE NEED to talk," Simone said halfway through her meal.

She'd whipped up fettuccine with a spicy sauce, a salad and garlic bread—one of Drew's favorite dinners. Not that anyone would know it, the way he was picking at his food.

"So talk," he said sullenly.

"It's you who needs to do the talking. Tell me what's bothering you."

She wasn't going to make the mistake of leading him, suggesting he should be upset by something he'd heard the night before.

"If you don't know, then it doesn't matter, does it?" He threw down his napkin and stood.

"Drew, sit. Finish eating."

"I lost my appetite. Maybe you can give the leftovers to your new boyfriend."

"Gideon isn't a boyfriend."

"Then what is he, Mom? I saw him kiss you. It was the middle of the night. I'm not naive. I'm seventeen."

Not quite. He was still sixteen, but she wasn't going to argue the point. She had to come up with something to explain Gideon.

She tactfully began, "It's difficult being alone so much when you're used to a man's company. David has been gone for quite a while now—"

"Eight lousy months. Charlie's mom waited longer than that after she divorced his dad."

A stab of relief shot through her. Was that it, then? Drew thought Gideon was her new boyfriend and he was upset because to him that meant she was cheating on his father?

"You're sure that's all that's bothering you?"

Drew looked at her, the cold glint in his eyes reminding her of Michael. "What else could it be, Mom? What else have you done?"

Without waiting for her to follow up on that, Drew turned and walked out of the kitchen. Trying to remain calm, Simone went after him.

"Drew, wait a minute."

But he kept going, right up the stairs, saying, "I'm done talking. I have to study."

So much for that conversation.

Frustrated, needing to talk to someone, Simone finally gave in to the urge to call Gideon. She knew he'd left her a couple of messages both at home and on her cell, which she'd turned off, so at least he wanted to talk to her.

Slipping on a jacket, she took her cell phone onto the back porch. The night was mild, the air winter-fresh, and she couldn't help the longing she felt to be enjoying it with Gideon standing behind her, his arms around her waist.

Pulse quickening at the fantasy, she placed a call to his cell.

"It's you," he answered. "I was wondering if you would return my calls."

"I was tied up."

"Literally?"

She thought to joke, then changed her mind and told him about "Santa Claus" attacking her that morning.

"Why didn't you call me?"

"I'm calling you now."

"I mean when it happened!"

"I wasn't sure if you wanted to hear from me."

"Because you left last night?"

Simone sighed. "I was trying to stay in control, Gideon. When I woke up, I realized I couldn't have that kind of complication in my life."

"Is that all I am to you? A complication?"

She wasn't about to tell him he was so much more, so she turned the conversation elsewhere. "I finally went to Cecchi and Burke this afternoon. I just got home."

"And?"

"I got two things. That half a mil from Anthony Viglio? Cash."

Gideon whistled. "Brave man, carrying that kind of

loot around. I assume people in the office remembered him."

"Apparently he only came once and the only one to see him was the receptionist. Her description—big and blond and blue-eyed."

"Not Anthony Viglio."

"Not by a long shot," she agreed. "But Sam Albright fits the description. And Ulf Nachtmann."

"Who?"

"Michael's bodyguard." Which worried her more than she wanted to admit.

"Albright had dealings with Cecchi, but I thought he was a satisfied customer. And wouldn't your receptionist have seen him more than once?"

"She's fairly new. Maybe not."

"And everyone else would simply have accepted Albright's presence without questioning his identity because they'd seen him before."

The logic made her feel a bit better. If Ulf were involved, it followed that Michael was, too, because where would a bodyguard get five hundred thousand dollars?

Gideon suddenly asked, "Any idea of what kind of car Sam Albright drives?"

"Some kind of a sedan, I think."

"Dark?"

"Black. Why?"

"Because someone driving a black sedan just tried to run me off the road," Gideon said.

"My God, how awful! What makes you think it was Sam Albright?"

"Whoever it was followed me from your place."

Stomach suddenly knotting—this was no coincidence—she asked, "What were you doing here?"

"I thought we needed to talk. I still do. Meet me out front in five minutes. I'm already on the way back to your place."

Simone didn't argue. His mind was made up. Besides, she wanted to see him for herself to make certain he was all right. No way was Sam Albright responsible. In her heart, she knew who was.

She banged at Drew's bedroom door and, without waiting for his invitation, showed herself in.

"What did you do, Drew?" she demanded. "What exactly did you hear last night?"

"I told you—"

"Not everything. Tell me. Now!"

"Okay. He's the guy who put Grandpa in prison," Drew said sullenly. "What are you doing with this guy, Mom? What are you doing with the man who betrayed this family?"

Simone grabbed the doorjamb for support and found herself defending him. "Gideon believed Papa killed his father. He did what he thought was right."

Isn't that what he had told her from the first? Why had she discounted it? Why had she pushed him out of her life?

Drew scowled, the expression so like Michael's it frightened her. "He lied!"

"He didn't lie."

"Now you're changing your story and saying Grandpa lied?"

"No!"

"It's got to be one or the other, Mom. One of them had to be lying. What other explanation is there?"

She'd thought the same thing, but she knew Gideon was convinced he'd been telling the truth.

"I don't know. What did you do, Drew? Who were you talking to on the phone last night?" she demanded as if she hadn't already figured it out.

"Uncle Mike!"

"Drew! We don't talk about it much, but you know your uncle can be a dangerous man." She'd have given anything not to be right about this. "A little while ago, Gideon almost had a car accident. Someone tried running him off the road."

"Uncle Mike is loyal to this family."

Without thinking, she snapped, "Gideon is your family, too! How can you think attacking him would be okay? I raised you to know right from wrong, Drew. Nothing justifies deliberately trying to hurt another person!"

"Gideon's not related to us!"

Realizing what she'd said, Simone knew now was the time for the whole truth. She'd been wrong to think that she could keep it from him...keep Gideon from the son he hadn't known existed.

Taking a deep breath, she said, "Gideon's related *to you,* Drew! He's your father, and your uncle knows that."

Drew flew off the bed, hands clenched at his sides. "My father's dead!"

"Yes, the man who raised you, the man who chose to be your father, who thought of you as a son and couldn't have loved you more—he *is* dead. Gideon is your *biological* father. He didn't even know about you until a few days ago. I was in love with him when his name was Joey Ruscetti, Drew. And I was pregnant with you when his father was murdered. If that hadn't happened…but it did, and nothing was ever the same again."

"I don't believe you!"

"I wouldn't lie to you about this."

Before she could think of some way of calming him down, Drew rushed past her out of the room.

"Drew, wait."

He flew down the stairs and grabbed his jacket.

She followed, asking, "Where are you going?"

"To the only person I can trust."

Chapter Fifteen

"I couldn't stop him from running to Michael."

Staring at Simone in the passenger seat—he'd picked her up in front of the house and had found a semi-deserted spot in nearby Lincoln Park to talk—Gideon was stunned.

"I can't believe you told him. You're the one who didn't want him to know that I'm his father. You were convinced it would destroy him."

"It may have, Gideon. You didn't see him," she said, a catch in her voice. "You didn't hear him."

"Take it easy. He'll be all right. He seems like a sensible kid."

"Usually."

"He will be this time, too. He's had a shock. He needs time to deal with what you told him."

"There's more."

Gideon didn't like the sound of that. "He didn't threaten to do anything to himself, did he?"

"No! The reason I told him about you…he was responsible for your close call earlier."

"You're saying he was driving the black sedan?"

She shook her head. "He told Michael about you. Last night he overheard us, at least enough to know that you were the man who put Papa behind bars."

Gideon cursed. He hadn't even gotten Simone out of the murder mess and now Michael was complicating the picture. He thought about facing down the man himself, but then thought better of it. If Michael had sent someone after him, it undoubtedly was already too late. Maybe he needed to talk to Logan, see if they could figure out a plan. Being a detective for the CPD, Logan might be the better person to approach Michael.

In the meantime…

"We need to find that tape." Gideon was certain that Simone had figured out what had been hidden in the desk. At least they now knew what to look for; they simply had to figure out who had possession of the tape. "Any ideas?"

"The murderer pretty much covered everyone who had access to the desk—Nikki, Galen, Josie, me."

"What about Teresa Cecchi?"

"What about her?"

"What if she knows something she hasn't told us?" Gideon suggested. "She *was* the last person to have her hands on the desk before it went to auction."

"Surely if she knew about the tape, she would have said something. Especially since she was so upset at the wake last night."

"You never mentioned that."

"I suggested that whatever had been in that desk was what got Al and Nikki killed. The idea shook her and she said their deaths were her fault. I just figured she was feeling guilty about giving away the desk. But maybe there's more to it."

"Only one way to find out." Knowing the wake had gone a second night, Gideon said, "She should be back from the funeral home by now."

"The funeral is tomorrow morning. I don't think she'll be happy to see us any time soon."

"From what I've seen, Teresa Cecchi is one tough widow. And if she has knowledge of the tape—or if she actually has the tape—we need to find out before someone else gets killed over the damned thing."

Simone agreed.

A quarter of an hour later, they were in front of the Cecchi home. The widow herself answered the door.

"What do you two want?"

"We want to know about the tape, Teresa," Simone said. "What's on it?"

"I—I don't know what you're talking about," the widow muttered as she tried to slam the door on them.

Quickly inserting a foot, Gideon prevented the door from being closed in their faces. "You can either talk to us, or you can talk to the authorities."

He could hardly believe that's all it had taken for Teresa Cecchi to cave. She must have been eaten up by guilt to give up so easily. Once inside, he noticed the woman's puffy eyes and smeared makeup and felt a pang of guilt. But what was done was done. Now they were getting somewhere, and keeping someone else from dying was more important than Teresa's feelings.

Simone asked, "What's on the tape, Teresa?"

"Information that could get us all killed."

"You knew this and didn't say anything?" Gideon asked.

"I thought if I pretended ignorance, it would protect me."

"From what?" Simone asked. "From whom?"

Teresa shook her head. "You won't like it."

"I don't have to like it if it helps nail Al's real killer."

Teresa nodded. "You'll have to hear for yourself."

The widow led them into the den and crossed the room to a painting. She pulled it from the wall, then opened the safe the artwork had hidden. She deftly punched in a code and the safe popped open. From the safe's depths, Teresa pulled an innocent-looking audio tape.

Gideon felt adrenaline surge through him. Teresa had warned Simone that she wasn't going to like what she would hear. Did that mean David Burke had been involved in something illegal?

But when Teresa inserted the tape into her sound system and hit Play, the voice on the tape wasn't David's. Even after all these years, Gideon recognized it immediately.

"I'll need you to keep him busy, so he doesn't suspect."

"Michael!" Simone said with a gasp.

Teresa stopped the tape. "I said you wouldn't like it."

"Play it!"

Teresa nodded and did as Simone demanded.

"As long as I don't have to get my hands dirty."

"You think they're clean, Al? You're the one who told me he was going to squeeze me out, get himself a new second-in-command."

"He's talking about Papa." Simone frowned. "Papa always demanded more, no matter how much Michael did for him. From the time Michael was a kid, Papa demanded he be a man."

"He doesn't trust you, Michael. Why should I?"

Michael laughed. "Maybe you should have taped this conversation for insurance."

"Th-that's not what I meant. I was talking about your funding my law firm. You are going to make good on that, right? I'll do like you say about handling any cases you want."

"Al, you think I'm gonna forget the person who helped make this possible?"

The last words slowed and then there was silence.

"Wait, there has to be more!" Simone cried. "What did he do?"

What had Michael done? Gideon wondered. Cecchi had taken care of the elder DeNali so Michael could what?

The dream vision came to him…

Pop and a man in an overcoat and brimmed hat, dark-framed glasses catching the light. A blue flash froze him to his seat as his father fell into the snow.

Still holding the gun, DeNali lit a cigarette with the other hand and got into his car and pulled away.

The license plate—RDN 1.

His father's eyes opened and slowly focused. "De-Nali…"

And then it hit him after all these years—the reason the dream wouldn't let him alone.

He flashed forward to the club the night of Cecchi's murder. He'd danced around Michael, kept his distance. He'd also kept an eye on the bastard, especially when Simone had stopped to talk to him. He remembered Michael had a drink in his right hand and with his left…

He bent a single match and touched the head to the flint, then flicked with his thumb so the match flamed to life.

Just like in the dream.

Pop had said *DeNali,* but hadn't said *Richard.*

"I'm sorry, that's all there was," Teresa Cecchi was saying when Gideon tuned back into the room.

Simone appeared devastated. No doubt she was drawing the same conclusions as he was. Gideon wrapped an arm around her shoulders to support her, and she slipped an arm around his waist. His chest squeezed tight at her returned gesture of solidarity.

"Are you sure there's no more later on the tape?" she asked as the widow withdrew it from the player.

"Positive. If you want to know the rest," Teresa said, "ask your brother."

"I'll do that."

As Simone pulled away from him, Gideon held out his hand. "The tape."

Teresa hesitated a moment, then handed it to him.

Gideon realized that Simone had left the room. He heard the whisper of footsteps rush down the hall and figured she needed a minute alone.

Slipping the tape into his pocket, he assured the widow, "I'll see that this gets into the right hands before someone else gets hurt."

Then he went after Simone. He expected to find her on the front porch, but she was already on the street at the car. The lights flashed and he realized she had his keys—she must have filched them from his pocket when she put her arm around his waist!

"Simone, what are you doing?" he demanded as she opened the driver's door. He was taking the steps two at a time. "Wait for me!"

But before he could get to her, she'd started the engine and was pulling away. Cursing, Gideon stood in the middle of the street knowing exactly where she was going. Following on foot—Michael lived barely a mile from here—he pulled out his cell and called Logan.

"I have what the murderer has been looking for," he said. "A tape. Michael DeNali was planning something against his father and Al Cecchi was involved."

"Planning what?"

"That's the question DeNali needs to answer." Though Gideon was certain he already knew.

As did Simone.

"You sound out of breath," Logan noted.

"I'm on the move on foot." Actually, he was jogging and finding speaking more difficult by the moment. "Simone took my car keys and she's on her way over to her brother's place right now. I could use some backup. Get over to the DeNali mansion on Eighteenth and Prairie."

"Will do."

Gideon slipped the cell back into his pocket and put on some speed.

THE STREET where Simone had spent her childhood was barely recognizable. A couple of decades ago, only a few houses that had belonged to the wealthy at the end of the nineteenth century were still being used as homes or businesses; the rest had stood empty. Most of the old buildings were gone now, replaced by a new housing development of three-story single-family homes, a condo complex and another construction site to the east.

"How am I going to do this with Drew there?" she said aloud.

Walls closed in on her mind as she pulled up in front of the mansion that had once been her home. Simone felt trapped by whatever truth Michael would tell her.

If he would tell her.

She had a moment's regret that she'd left Gideon behind. He'd been her rock over the past few days, and she knew he could get her through this. But his being here now could get him killed; given that possibility, she'd made the only decision she could. Michael would never hurt her, but Gideon was another story. He'd said her brother had come after him years ago—the reason he'd left his mother and sister for their own protection and had gone off on his own.

She'd assumed Michael had been seeking vengeance for their father, but in truth, he'd probably been trying to eliminate the only witness.

Swallowing the bile that rose to her throat, Simone left the car and ran up the front steps. Anger made her hammer at the bell continuously until the door opened.

To her surprise, Michael, rather than Ulf, stood on the other side.

"Come in. What's got you so hot?"

She pushed past him and through the foyer, looking for her son in either of the downstairs parlors, throwbacks to another age with marble fireplaces, parquet floors, oak-paneled walls and Tiffany windows. Both rooms were empty.

Feeling hot and cold at the same time, she faced her brother. "Is Drew upstairs in bed?"

"Drew? What makes you think he's here?"

"He's not?"

"I haven't seen him. I swear. You two have a big fight or something?"

"Or something," Simone agreed, wondering what in the world had happened to her son. perhaps he'd come to his senses and returned home. "Thanks to you."

She didn't miss the whisper of knowledge that flitted through Michael's expression before he covered it.

"I don't know what you're talking about, Sis."

"The past, bro! It's all about the past!"

Michael crossed his arms over his chest and leaned against the jamb of the north parlor's pocket door. He was trying to look casual, Simone thought. Innocent. She could read him like a book.

"Want to be more specific?" he asked.

"Who did you order to run Gideon off the road earlier, Michael? Was it Ulf? Or someone else on your so-called security team?"

"If you think Ulf did something he shouldn't have, I'll speak to him about it."

"This is me you're talking to, Michael. I heard the tape you've been searching for. I know what you are now!"

Michael lunged from the doorway, shouting, "I'm your brother, head of this family!"

Simone stood her ground and glared at him in return. "If you think that guarantees you respect, you're wrong! You have to *earn* respect, not steal it by taking someone's life and making it look like your own father is the murderer."

Silence but for the grandfather clock in the foyer. Tick…tick…tick…

Simone watched her brother's face turn to stone. He didn't even try to deny it. So it was true—he'd been the DeNali who had killed Frank Ruscetti. He'd dressed in Papa's clothes and glasses, had driven Papa's car. What else had Gideon been left to think when he'd seen the shooting, especially when with his dying breath, his father had uttered *DeNali?*

Both he and Papa had told the truth under oath…

The Michael who could orchestrate this was a stranger to her. Simone's eyes filled with tears as she glared at him. "How, Michael? How could you do this?"

"The old man deserved it. You know he did."

"He loved us."

"He loved you. Me, he treated like dirt. Said he would make a man out of me no matter what he had to do. Well, he finally succeeded, didn't he? He was going to replace me, Simone, like I was nothing! He pushed me too far that time. He should really be proud of what I did."

"You're proud of setting him up?"

"I thought it was a clever plan. I even arranged it so Joey Ruscetti could see the action. One of my men let me know when he dropped you off, then followed Joey and let me know when he was within home radar."

"My God, you're heartless! You killed Frank Ruscetti—"

"A known criminal."

"—in front of his son!" Simone exclaimed. "And Al Cecchi wasn't a criminal and neither was Nikki Albright!"

"Maybe not Nikki, but Al's another story. He helped me, didn't he? And what do you call what Al did with the firm's money? Besides, I didn't kill them."

"I suppose you weren't after the tape, either," she said, remembering her tussle with Santa. Had Michael really meant to hurt her, as well? Perhaps kill her?

"I didn't even know about the tape until recently, when Al decided to blackmail me. He whined and said he needed the money to replace firm funds that he'd gambled away before he was investigated. He was stupid enough to hide the original tape in that damn desk his wife gave away. He was supposed to get it and give it to Ulf."

"Ulf."

"I wasn't there when Al Cecchi was murdered, Simone. I was with Josie Ralston, I swear."

"You're saying Ulf is the murderer?"

"You assumed it was me?" Michael sounded offended. "When Al couldn't come up with the tape, Ulf got carried away."

"And Nikki?"

"Apparently she caught him the act of ripping the desk apart."

Footsteps from the back of the house spurred Simone to see who was there. Ulf filled the doorway to the dining room and library.

"Don't try to play innocent with your sister, Michael," the bodyguard said. "You told me to do whatever I needed to do to get the tape."

"Not murder."

"Why not? *You've* murdered for it."

"Enough!" Michael roared.

"And now it's time for you to pay."

Realizing that Ulf didn't mean Frank Ruscetti, Simone asked, "What is he saying?"

But either Michael didn't hear her or he was ignoring her. His gaze glued to his bodyguard, he said, "We'll talk about this later."

"Now!" Ulf insisted. "Your sister knows, so this Gideon must know. And it follows that the police will know soon if not already. Time for me to disappear."

"Michael, who did you murder?" Simone asked, her voice shrill enough to make both men turn toward her.

"Simone, I think you'd better leave!" Michael snapped.

"Not until I get my money." Ulf pulled a gun. "No one leaves until then. Half a million dollars will do me for a while."

Michael began, "I don't have it—"

"Ask him how your husband died."

"Ulf!"

Simone looked from bodyguard to her brother. "Michael, what is he talking about?"

Her brother was stone-silent. Not so his bodyguard.

"Apparently your husband got a whiff of the money missing from the firm and went through Cecchi's office to find out why his partner would cheat him. Cecchi had been making copies of the tape he used to blackmail Michael and left one in the sound system. Your husband listened to it and came here to talk to Michael, demanding the whole truth."

Simone's eyes widened and she gasped, "Michael, no!"

Her brother looked shamefaced but defended himself. "I had to do it, Simone. He was going to go to the authorities. I offered him money, but he wouldn't take it. I did the only thing I *could* do."

Simone felt faint. *David!* Dear Lord, no. "You're the one who drove David off the road?"

"He left me no choice."

"And you tried to do the same to Gideon tonight!" The room started spinning around her and she latched on to a chair for support.

"My money!" Ulf demanded. When Michael didn't

respond, he sighed. "I see you need incentive." He backed to the hall door and without taking the gun off them, swung it open to reveal a body crumpled on the floor.

"Drew!" Simone said with a gasp as Ulf dragged him to his feet. She started to move toward her son, but the killer waved her off with his gun.

Drew's hands were tied behind his back, a gag covered his mouth and his knees were wobbly. The wild look in his eyes told Simone he'd probably overheard everything. She had to get herself together for his sake.

"After all I've done for you, you betray me by threatening my family?" Michael spat. "Let the boy go! Now!"

"You don't give the orders anymore. The boy for the money."

"No, please," Simone begged, moving closer to the gun, which was now trained on her. Surely fate wouldn't be so cruel as to take her son. She couldn't let it happen. "Drew's innocent in all this. He's just a boy! Let him go and take me, instead, please!"

"Stay back!" Ulf ordered, taking aim when she didn't listen and kept coming.

"Simone, no!" Michael shouted, throwing himself between her and the bullet that exploded from the gun's barrel.

Chapter Sixteen

"Michael!"

Simone's shrill scream set Gideon's neck hair on edge. Circling the building, he finally found a way in through the back, where a door stood open. Still out of breath—probably the fastest mile he'd ever run—he slipped into the darkened room and edged toward the voices.

"Get out, Ulf, before the police get here," Simone said, her voice breaking with anguish. "Someone will have heard that gun go off."

"Yeah, maybe. But who will care?" the bodyguard asked.

Gideon tiptoed from what proved to be the kitchen into a hallway and stiffened. Ahead, the bodyguard's back was to him. The bastard had Drew! The boy was struggling, but obviously had been hurt or drugged because he appeared woozy. Ulf held him up by the arm with one hand and with the other waved a gun at Simone, who knelt on the floor next to Michael. Her hands shook as she felt for his pulse. Red bloomed from a bullet hole in the man's shoulder; he looked next to dead, Gideon thought.

Simone looked up at Ulf with a hopeful expression. "Michael's still alive! I have to call 911!"

"Not until I have my money," Ulf told her. "Your brother keeps stacks of bills in the safe. I've seen them."

"I don't have the combination."

"That's too bad. You'd better figure out a way to open the damn thing before he dies. And, oh, yeah, if I don't have money in three minutes, the kid gets it, too."

As if staring at Simone willed her to look his way, she did. Gideon saw recognition light her eyes before she turned her gaze back to Ulf. Hope laced her expression, and Gideon knew she was going to try something, so he went on the alert.

"All right, I'll try some possible combinations of numbers," she said, scrambling to her feet. "Maybe Michael used one of our birthdates. But you have to give me some time."

"Tick tock!" Stepping forward and dragging Drew with him, Ulf waved the gun at her.

"Wait a minute!" she cried, stopping suddenly. "What did you do to my son?"

"He'll be—"

Before Ulf could finish, Gideon rammed himself between them, making him let go of Drew.

"Try picking on someone your own size!" Gideon growled as he chopped down into Ulf's hand so the gun went spinning down the hallway.

"My pleasure!"

Ulf lowered his shoulder and rammed Gideon square in the chest. The air knocked out of him, Gideon flew backward and couldn't catch himself. His back bounced against a doorjamb and he fell to one knee.

Ulf wasted no time in going after the gun.

And Simone wasted no time trying to beat him to it.

Ulf grabbed her arm, whipped her around and smashed his fist into her middle. Simone crumpled. Furious, Gideon launched himself at the man just as Ulf was about to snatch up the gun. They rolled into the south parlor, fists flying.

Ulf tried taking out Gideon's nose with the heel of his hand, but Gideon was faster. He caught Ulf's hand and snapped it back so fast the bodyguard shrieked and rolled away, only to face Simone, who now had his gun in her hand, pointed at his chest.

For a big man, Ulf was fast. He flew to his feet and out the front door.

Gideon was right behind him.

The killer was nearly to the bottom of the stairs. Gideon jumped and hit the man with his legs from behind. They both went down on the sidewalk. Ulf elbowed back hard enough to make Gideon let go and then scrambled out from under him. But Gideon caught his leg and twisted. The other man landed on his back and struck out with his free leg, shoving a foot into Gideon's head. The world whirled and for a moment, he couldn't move.

Free again, Ulf scrambled to his feet and ran. Forcing himself to focus, Gideon rose and stumbled after him.

He caught up to Ulf as he tried to jump the wrought iron fence into the park that edged a couple of historic houses. Gideon dragged him down hard so his clothing caught on the spikes. Ulf dangled there, limbs flailing ineffectually, as a blue and white turned the corner, lights flashing. Another car—one Gideon recognized—followed.

Logan had arrived with backup.

LESS THAN twenty-four hours later, Simone uncovered the boxes of ornaments that she'd been ignoring for the last week. She set them on the tables near the Christmas tree, stopping to hold one that reminded her of David. They'd picked this one out together as a souvenir of a skiing vacation. Her eyes filled with tears at the thought of his unnecessary death, a death caused by her own brother.

Michael had survived emergency surgery and she was thankful for that. Police officers now guarded his hospital room. Michael would be standing trial on multiple counts. Simone knew he deserved whatever punishment he got. Who knew if justice would truly be served? The tape had led her and Gideon to figure out his deception in Frank Ruscetti's murder, but would it be enough to convict him? There was no proof that he'd killed David. No witness. Only hearsay. Hers. Drew's. And of course Ulf had already turned on his employer to lighten his own sentence.

Simone hated the fact that she might have to testify against her own brother. Michael had done terrible things, had taken lives, but in the end had risked his own to save hers. He'd always been there for her in his twisted way; even if her testimony put him away, she would be there for him if he could stand the sight of her.

No matter what he had done, some part of her still loved him.

Just as she loved her father, who, if the justice system worked the way it should, would soon be released from prison.

"Hey, Mom, I thought you said he was coming," Drew said, entering the living room, hands shoved deep into his chino pockets.

Was that an anxious note in his voice?

Just as she said, "He'll be here," the doorbell rang. "I'll get it."

She watched Drew open the door and then back off. He was anxious but not eager to show it.

Gideon entered and nodded to his son, then handed him two gaily wrapped presents. "Can you put these someplace safe until we get the tree decorated?"

"Yeah, sure." Drew took them and surreptitiously inspected the tags before setting them down on the fireplace mantle.

Simone smiled.

She would never have thought this was possible— the three of them being in the same room together, decorating for a holiday, no less. But after hearing Michael's admissions the night before, Drew reluctantly agreed that he would be willing to get to know Gideon better. Perhaps he hadn't fully accepted Gideon as his father—perhaps, out of loyalty to David, he never would—but this was a promising start.

Her heart filled as they decorated the tree, talking and laughing together, Christmas music in the background, logs in the fireplace popping.

Simone reached out to straighten a string of lights and Gideon's hand knocked into hers as he tried to do the same. A thrill shot through her that spoke of an intimacy that had nothing to do with sex. And when the last ornament was in place and Gideon had declared it a masterpiece, Simone thought she'd never seen such a beautiful tree.

"Mom made cookies before you got here," Drew told Gideon. "If you want, I can make some hot chocolate to go with them."

"Sounds good."

Simone could only describe Gideon's expression as loopy as he watched his son head for the kitchen.

"A good start," she murmured.

"I never thought…"

"Me, neither."

They fell into a comfortable silence for a moment. *Then…*

"What about you?" Gideon asked. "Can you ever forgive me for putting the wrong man in prison?"

"Michael is the one to blame, not you. You didn't lie. Both you and Papa did tell the truth, after all. There's nothing to forgive. I never should have abandoned you."

"Sometimes things work out the way they need to," Gideon said. "I can tell how much you cared about David. And he helped you raise a great kid. How could I wish that away?"

Simone blinked fast—she didn't want tears to spoil the moment. "Thank you."

"The thing is, what about when he gets out? Will you still be willing to see me then?"

"I love my family, but I don't plan on letting anyone run my life again."

"So after everything that's happened, we stand a chance together?"

Simone nodded. "But let's take it slow, let Drew get used to you."

Gideon grinned at her and she could tell he was about to kiss her when, from the kitchen, Drew yelled, "Hot chocolate and cookies coming up."

They laughed together instead, and as their son entered the room carrying a tray, Simone knew her heart couldn't feel fuller.

Epilogue

"So the dream did have meaning," Cass mused, nodding as Team Undercover hashed out the details of the case in Gideon's office.

"Freaky," Gideon said. "The way Michael lit that cigarette one-handed so he could keep the gun in the other was there all along, and I just wasn't able to zoom in on it until it was almost too late."

"*Almost* is the key word," Gabe said.

"We caught up with Josie Ralston. She took off for a few days, so she wasn't around when Ulf Nachtmann got into her apartment. Since DeNali took up with her, I figure he had keys to her place. So Ulf got 'em from DeNali's stash." Logan flicked an invisible fleck from his suit lapel. "Doesn't look like she did anything she can be held accountable for. And I don't think she's gonna be returning any of the law firm's funds."

"Once Simone gives a copy of the official report to the company that insured David, she and Drew will be set," Gideon said.

"Besides, they have *you* now."

Gideon grinned at Cass.

Blade opened a bottle of champagne—they always toasted their successes.

"To the next poor soul who needs us," Gabe said, lifting his glass.

"Success!" they all chimed in.

A rock version of a Christmas tune blasted from the club. Gideon had been humming Christmas carols himself since decorating the tree with Simone and Drew. They were going to attend church together on Christmas Eve, and he was invited to Christmas dinner. It had been too many years since he'd been with family for the holidays.

In his mind, this was one red carpet Christmas.

Holiday to-do list:

- wrap gifts
- catch a thief
- solve a murder
- deal with Mom

Well-respected Florida detective Maggie Skerritt
is finally getting her life on track when a
suspicious crime shakes up her holiday plans.

Holidays Are Murder
Charlotte Douglas

KELSEY ROBERTS
CHARMED AND DANGEROUS

When FBI agent J. J. Barnes is assigned to a high
profile investigation, the last person she wants
to be paired with is the arrogant Cody Landry.
But after succumbing to their heated passion
J. J. must make a choice…back out now or
risk her heart with a possible suspect.

Also watch for

THE LAST LANDRY, March 2006

Available wherever Harlequin Books are sold.

If you enjoyed what you just read,
then we've got an offer you can't resist!

Take 2 bestselling love stories FREE!

Plus get a FREE surprise gift!

Clip this page and mail it to Harlequin Reader Service®

IN U.S.A.	**IN CANADA**
3010 Walden Ave.	P.O. Box 609
P.O. Box 1867	Fort Erie, Ontario
Buffalo, N.Y. 14240-1867	L2A 5X3

YES! Please send me 2 free Harlequin Intrigue® novels and my free surprise gift. After receiving them, if I don't wish to receive anymore, I can return the shipping statement marked cancel. If I don't cancel, I will receive 4 brand-new novels each month, before they're available in stores! In the U.S.A., bill me at the bargain price of $4.24 plus 25¢ shipping and handling per book and applicable sales tax, if any*. In Canada, bill me at the bargain price of $4.99 plus 25¢ shipping and handling per book and applicable taxes**. That's the complete price and a savings of at least 10% off the cover prices—what a great deal! I understand that accepting the 2 free books and gift places me under no obligation ever to buy any books. I can always return a shipment and cancel at any time. Even if I never buy another book from Harlequin, the 2 free books and gift are mine to keep forever.

181 HDN DZ7N
381 HDN DZ7P

Name	(PLEASE PRINT)	
Address	Apt.#	
City	State/Prov.	Zip/Postal Code

Not valid to current Harlequin Intrigue® subscribers.

Want to try two free books from another series?
Call 1-800-873-8635 or visit www.morefreebooks.com.

* Terms and prices subject to change without notice. Sales tax applicable in N.Y.
** Canadian residents will be charged applicable provincial taxes and GST.
   All orders subject to approval. Offer limited to one per household.
   ® are registered trademarks owned and used by the trademark owner and or its licensee.

INT04R   ©2004 Harlequin Enterprises Limited

HOMICIDE DETECTIVE
MERRI WALTERS IS BACK IN

Silent Reckoning
by Debra Webb

December 2005

A serial killer was on the loose,
hunting the city's country singers.
Could deaf detective Merri Walters turn
her hearing loss to advantage and crack
the case before the music died?

Available at your favorite retail outlet.